I0542309

BEST BEHAVIOUR

MATTHEW J. METZGER

BEST BEHAVIOUR

Chapter One

By the time Jim swallowed his pride, he was standing on the pavement with three bin bags and an overgrown spider plant.

"Can you come over?" he asked. "I need your help." Then he hung up.

Sarah rang back, of course, but Jim didn't answer. He just sat down on one of the bags, put the plant down next to his boot and leaned back against the railings.

Fuck.

That was the only thing that came to mind. *Fuck.* How the fuck had he ended up — well, no, he knew exactly how he'd ended up like this. Stupidity and pride and a whole host of other things that weren't all that flattering. And yet, even as he combed through them all in his head, he'd not change any of them. So, what did that make him?

At least it wasn't raining.

Stretching out his legs in front of him, Jim examined his tatty boots and absently wondered if he ought to try building sites. But even they needed certificates and shit these days. Only thing Jim knew how to do was put boxes on shelves and say, "Would you like fries with that?"

And even the places that sold fries didn't want him.

It wasn't that he hadn't tried. They'd known for months that the warehouse was going to fold eventually, and he'd been looking for other work. But everywhere asked for qualifications. And the places that didn't took one look at his history — specifically that weird little gap after that night with the car — and told him to get packing.

Well, he was packed now.

Whole life in three bin bags. And a plant. Great success he'd made of himself there. Wouldn't Mum be proud?

He snorted. No doubt Sarah would pass the message along.

He wanted nothing less than to have to ring Sarah, but he was out of options. If he ended up in a cardboard box on the streets — or, worse, a Sally Army hostel — then he *would* end up back in prison. Knew it just as much as he knew the sky was blue. And even his pride wasn't so huge as to want to go crawling back in there.

Still —

He'd had a plan, when he got out. Sort himself out. Get a job, find a flat, settle down with the right eight or ten people he'd like to shag for the rest of eternity. Sounded easy, when there were several hundred odd days to think about it in a cell. Only the right person hadn't been right after all. And the job hadn't lasted. And the flat needed the job.

Chewing on a corner of his thumb, Jim sighed. At least the bailiffs wouldn't be on first name terms with him anymore.

A silver Merc came creeping around the end of the road. It looked absurdly out of place in Jim's road full of burned-out Clios and old Skodas with black alloy wheels. It shimmered like a police car as it inched toward him and stopped right across the entrance to the flats as if it owned the lot of them. Driver probably could have *bought* the lot of them.

Jim lifted a hand and waved.

The driver's door opened. A ridiculously tall heel landed on the potholed tarmac and a slim woman unfolded herself from the car. She frowned down at him like a scolding parent or a disappointed probation officer and Jim could have laughed. She looked more like either of those than what she was.

"Hey, sis."

"What happened?" Sarah asked.

She didn't greet him. She certainly didn't hug him. Strip back all the pretence and they would have looked very alike—both tall, both with honey-coloured hair, both with the glass-cutting jawline. But Sarah's hair was in a perfect bun, her suit pristine, her nails gleaming. She hadn't even been working today, but that was how a mum of three *could* look when she hired a nanny. Then there was Jim—hunched over, hands in pockets, hair on end, unshaven, still wearing his hi-vis vest and dirty jeans as if he had a job.

Like peas in a mile-long pod.

"Lost my job," he said.

"Again?"

"We all did," he said defensively. "They've closed the warehouse."

Her frown eased a fraction.

"Then came home and the landlord was here. Said if I couldn't cough up five hundred by Friday he'd evict me. So I told him about the job, and" — Jim gestured to his spider plant — "here I am."

There was a long, long silence.

So long, in fact, that ice ages came and went. Evolution spawned four hundred new species. Mars underwent a century of its own. The big bang began to revert into the big crunch.

Then Sarah said, "Why did you owe your landlord five hundred pounds?"

"And the rest."

"What?"

"I owed him a grand and a half."

Her jaw dropped. "You *what?*"

Jim shrugged.

"Why weren't you paying your rent!"

"With what?" Jim asked. "They cut the gas off last week. I owe water like…four hundred and something. Even the bank's started threatening with bailiffs. I'm out of options. Why d'you think I rang you?"

Her jaw was still agape, but she spluttered.

"Four hun — the bank — *bailiffs?*"

"Yeah."

He felt about an inch tall and his stomach was clenching up. He was too hot. His leg started to jiggle.

"Why didn't you ask me for help?"

"I did. Am."

"Sooner than being — you've been evicted!"

The hot feeling boiled over. "Right. Yeah. Because asking worked so well last time."

"That was different."

"It really wasn't," he replied tightly. "That was *worse* than this."

She pursed her lips, eyeing his spider plant. It looked sorry for itself on the grubby flagstones. But to hell with her and her demands. She hadn't helped when he'd asked the first time. Why would he ask again?

"I tried everything," he said. "But today was the last straw. So here I am."

"Here you are," she echoed weakly, then shook herself. "Right. Well. Our spare room it is."

He grimaced but said nothing. The truth was, Jim didn't want Sarah's help or Sarah's spare room. He'd tried everyone else while the landlord had been flinging his things in the bin. Old work colleagues who didn't want to know. An ex-boyfriend who'd asked, "Who?" as though Jim had vanished out of existence when they'd split up. He'd even tried Justin, much as he didn't want to be around that smug fucker with his new fiancé.

But, in the end, nobody had been able — or wanted — to help.

So here he was, squinting up at Sarah in the dying light.

"Come on," she said. "Let's get that lot in the boot."

She didn't touch the bags. She just opened the boot and held the plant on her hip like a baby as he moved them. The smackheads over the road were staring and he flipped them off as he banged the lid down.

"Jim! This is a new car!"

"Sorry," he muttered.

"Let me just call Anthony…"

Jim rolled his eyes, unable to help himself. "I'm sure this'll go down really well."

She raised an eyebrow. "Don't you go bringing him into this."

"Why not?" he asked. "You brought him into it last time."

"It wasn't like that."

"Really, because it sure felt like that."

"Well, it wasn't."

Jim rolled his eyes but gave up. He wished he could end arguments like that. He wished his interpretation of events was the definitive one. What it must be like, to have that kind of power? But then he'd never had that power with Sarah. He doubted anyone ever did.

He let himself into the passenger seat as she talked on her phone and sulked in the front like a little kid. His skin itched. His stomach was a lump of lead. He desperately didn't want to be doing this—but it was just temporary, he told himself. Just until he could find another job. A better job. Longer hours and higher pay.

It was a short chat. She waved her hands a lot. And eventually she hung up and got into the driver's seat, mouth tight as though they'd argued.

"Told you he wouldn't like it."

"Enough, please."

Jim shut his mouth and stared at the flats as Sarah turned the car around, and they slowly vanished in the wing mirror.

"I didn't realise things had gotten this bad. You should have talked to me."

Jim grunted.

"You should have talked to Mum."

"Oh, right, yeah—"

"She's just worried about you."

"She screens her calls. She won't answer. Hasn't since I came out."

"I'm sure she—"

"Don't tell me what Mum means," Jim said tightly. "You weren't there. You didn't hear her. I know exactly what she means."

An uneasy silence fell between them. Sarah clenched and relaxed her fingers around the steering wheel in an anxious rhythm, and Jim's leg was jiggling again.

"How good did you think it was?" he asked quietly. "I'm eight grand in debt and I worked minimum wage. What did you think was happening?"

"I don't want to talk about that," she snapped.

It was all she'd ever said since that original no. She didn't want to talk about it. She never wanted to talk about it. If Jim brought it up, she changed the subject. Left up to Sarah, they'd *never* talk about it.

"I would have helped if you'd told me," she said after a while and Jim snorted.

"Since when do you *help?*" he demanded.

She pursed her lips. "Since always. You were just too stubborn to see it."

His jaw ached and he realised that he was grinding his teeth again. Slowly, he relaxed his jaw. He couldn't afford to piss her off now. He'd have to be on his best behaviour, at least until he found another job.

But it was a mutinous silence. Because the rub was that Sarah had been right. Anthony had refused to help because he was a judgemental prick, but Sarah had done this pragmatic refusal that had hurt worse, somehow. Religious bigotry, Jim could kind of roll with that. Anthony was dumb as his dog collar anyway—what did Jim expect?

But Sarah? Sarah's practicality had *hurt.*

And, worse still, it had been *right.*

So he seethed quietly as they left the city behind. The traffic was busy, commuters rushing home from their better jobs to their better homes with their partners and kids, not their sisters and crap in-laws. He stared out at the sea of other people as they inched away to the south and wondered if he'd ever get on track. Sarah had only four years on him, but she had it all figured out. Jim…Jim felt as if he'd been careering from one disaster to another ever since he was a kid.

And bleeding away into the wide avenues, long driveways and conservatories of Dore and Totley didn't help. Sarah fitted in out here. Her Merc, her suit, her manicure drumming ceaselessly on the leather. Jim felt like he had in prison and sank lower and lower in his seat as they left even the outskirts behind and dipped into the countryside proper.

The house lay just shy of the Derbyshire border — Jim could just about see the sign — and the electric gates were a foreboding barrier against the likes of him. The place screamed money. Gated drive. Detached twin garage. A summerhouse visible round the side. Since Jim had last been — when Agnes was born, over a year ago now — they'd had an honest-to-God fountain installed in front of the steps that led up to the front door.

It was more like a mansion than someplace people actually *lived*.

"It's been a while," he said uselessly as Sarah tucked the Merc into the garage next to a gleaming BMW on the latest plates.

"Yes."

"How's everyone?"

"Oh, they're fine."

Another long pause. Jim lifted his bin bags. Sarah took the plant. Then he was looking up at the house and he wanted to scream.

"Come on," she said. "I'll show you which room you can have. And you'll join us for dinner, won't you?"

"Not really that hung —"

"Of course you will," she interrupted as she opened the door. A bell chimed. "Zoe! Zoe, are you in?"

Jim was listening.

He stood in the hall and stared at the spiral stairs sweeping away to the first floor like something out of a wedding brochure. At the marble floor. At the chandelier. At the two-storey windows dominating the back of the hall and showing the gardens falling away to the south of the house. At the money oozing off the walls — and at the white dog collar, sitting proudly on a hook by a collection of tidy coats and above a rack of expensive shoes.

Forget Zoe. Anthony was home.

And this was going to be hell on earth.

Chapter Two

Jim stayed in his room as long as humanly possible.

It was in the attic. There were three small rooms up there, and a bathroom. If slavery were legal, he had no doubt it would be where the staff were kept — but thankfully the nanny, Zoe, lived in a room next to the nursery and he had the attic area to himself.

Christ, his sister had a nanny. What thirty-year-old woman had a *nanny?*

That was the bit that grated the most. Sarah was only thirty. She was only four years older than him. She acted as though she were forty, but Jim remembered her wearing her primary school pleated skirts and learning to read. He remembered her as a kid. As a gobby teenager. Slamming doors and shouting she hated Mum and dying her hair pink to annoy the teachers at school.

Then she'd gone off to university and done exactly what he had — and hadn't — expected.

He had expected the six-figure salary and the power suit. They were why she'd gone. She was already a marketing executive of a major firm. One day she'd be CEO. And, when the kids were in their teens and she didn't have to pay the damn nanny so much, she'd go off and become an MP. Jim had expected all that.

Except for the kids bit.

Except for the bit where she'd gotten married at nineteen, before she'd even finished her first year.

Except for the bit where she'd married *Anthony*.

Jim had always expected Sarah to be one of those never-needed-a-man types—and if she ever got married, it would be to some high-flying business or politics type. Someone like her. She'd be one half of one of those power-couples. Instead she'd gone off to university at eighteen and been married and an expectant mum by nineteen.

To the reverend at Mum's church.

Anthony Lovelace—formerly Anthony Lacey, but like hell Sarah was just taking her husband's last name without a fight—had been the reverend at Mum's new church when she'd moved to her bungalow to retire. And Anthony wasn't one of those new young vicars trying to make the church sexy again. He was fifty-one.

Jim's nineteen-year-old sister had married a fifty-one-year-old reverend.

And if that part hadn't made Jim uncomfortable enough, getting to know his brother-in-law hadn't helped matters. The man was a posh upper-class twassock with a public school education and a degree from the University of Cambridge. He was also fanatically boring. His hobbies included fishing. Not *going* fishing but watching it. On the TV. For hours on end.

A stuffy old reverend was the last person Jim wanted to be around at the best of times and the way that Anthony looked at him just made things worse. It wasn't even disgust or hatred. It was *pity*. The man looked at him the way Jim looked at those adverts of starving kiddies in Africa between comedy stand-up shows on the telly. Anthony looked at him as if he felt sorry for Jim all the time. Poor Jim, being an atheist and not clever enough to have faith. Poor Jim, being bisexual and afflicted with a terrible sin. Poor Jim, being no better than a horny dog and having a better knowledge of bondage than bibles.

God, he wanted to punch that morose face every time he saw it.

Which was why he tried to wait dinner out in his new room, but eventually Sarah came up to get him and he was dragged down for dinner like an erstwhile kid. Which — of course — brought him face-to-face with said stuffy reverend.

"Oh," Anthony said. "Yes. James."

"Jim."

Anthony looked like someone's granddad. Or Anthony Hopkins gone to seed. But the little kids around the table were his kids, not his grandkids. Ten-year-old Oscar didn't even look up from his plate to say hello. Six-year-old Patricia stared curiously over her already badly mauled fish. The only person who looked happy to be there was Agnes, and given that she was only a baby, that could probably be forgiven.

"Hi, Aggie," Jim said, clasping her pudgy fist between finger and thumb to wave it and beaming at her when she giggled.

Anthony gave him a sour look and rose to his feet.

"A quick word, please, James?"

Jim rolled his eyes but followed him into the cavernous kitchen. When the reverend rounded on

him, Jim lounged back against the counter in his most
obnoxiously laddish pose.

"I don't suppose Sarah's gone over the ground
rules?"

"Nope."

"If you could refrain from nicknaming the children,
we would appreciate it. The girls are at an
impressionable age and we prefer to teach them to
respect one's names."

Jim raised his eyebrows. "She's a toddler. I can't call
a toddler Aggie?"

"I would prefer you used her name."

"Right..."

"And if you could keep the, ah, language to a
minimum, that would be appreciated as well."

"I said hi!"

"I ask in anticipation."

"Of course you do."

"There is also the—ah—matter of your..."

He trailed off. Jim raised his eyebrows and folded
his arms over his chest.

"My what?"

"Well."

"My *what?*"

"Your—"

Another long silence. Jim knew full well what the
next word would be, or at least what it would mean.

"If you could avoid from bringing men into the
house—"

"What about women?"

Anthony hesitated.

"Right," Jim said. "Can we go eat?"

"I don't mean anything by it—"

"Can we go and eat?" Jim asked loudly.

Anthony pinked at the volume but nodded. He waved a hand to the door and Jim stalked back into the dining room. Patricia was still gawping. Oscar looked as if he'd heard every word and wanted to sink under the table. Anthony and Sarah, though, were supremely unruffled, as though nothing had happened — even though Jim wanted to deck the pair of them. Christ, couldn't go an hour in the house without someone trotting out some bigoted bullshit.

"Let us say grace."

Jim was too petty to take part and pulled faces at his giggly little niece all the way through the prayer. When it was over, he poked the fish dubiously and hoped that if he kept his head down, dinner would go without any stupid comments from the old fart at the head of the table.

"So, James."

So much for that.

"Sarah says that you're out of work."

"Yep."

"I'm sorry to hear you're struggling."

"Yep."

"You can stay here as long as you need to."

"Yep."

"Is Uncle James staying?" Patricia asked, eyeing him keenly across the table. Like him and Sarah, she was blonde, and had big dark eyes. Slightly less like them — he hoped — she had the murderous look of a tiny psychopath as she impaled her fish on her fork with incredible force, the shriek of metal on china deafening.

"Yes," Sarah said.

"Why?"

"Because he's fallen on hard times," Anthony said. "Don't talk while you're eating."

Patricia obediently fell quiet but eyeballed Jim with psychotic intensity. He swore she didn't blink as she slowly tore the fish into a thousand pieces, and never took her eyes off him as she sank her little teeth into the overcooked flesh.

He shivered.

Christ. If the brother-in-law didn't get him, the niece might.

* * * *

Jim woke up late.

The room he'd been given was a lacy nightmare, but at least the bed was comfortable. The sun poked him in the eyes and he could faintly hear a piano. When he rolled over and checked his watch on the nightstand, it was ten past eleven.

Christ, he'd needed that sleep.

At least it was a Friday. Kids would be at school. Sarah would be at work. Anthony would be — doing whatever reverends did during the week. He could pilfer some breakfast out of the fridge, then find a decent hiding spot. Or the Wi-Fi password.

He made use of the obscenely fluffy towels in the bathroom before getting dressed and heading downstairs, combing his wet hair into spikes as he went. The piano was getting louder. Jim didn't have much of an ear for music, but it sounded complicated. Clashy. Lots of banging, but not in a way that suggested a shit piano player. Pianist. Whatever. He wondered if it was the nanny.

Hm, he hadn't actually seen Zoe. Maybe she was cute. Some young French student paying her way for a master's, something classy like that. Pretty and well-educated and up for a bit of rough like Jim. Up for some fun. That would really piss Anthony off, if Jim could have his end away with the hired help.

So once he'd inhaled a pint of milk and some handfuls of cereal out of a new box in the kitchen, Jim went searching for that ceaseless, energetic music and — hopefully — its energetic player, too.

Thing was, he didn't really remember much about Sarah's house from Aggie's christening. And he wasn't the best with sound. Mum used to say he was hard of hearing and it was true Jim struggled with understanding voices in busy rooms or figuring out where a sound was coming from. The piano sounded as though it could be in every single room on the ground floor and so he ended up trying almost every door in the place before finally finding a study or drawing room at the front of the house, just off from the living room, and finding a deluge of classical piano.

He edged around the door — and stopped dead.

There was an angel sitting at the piano.

Sunlight was streaming through the bay window, casting a halo around the piano and its player. It burned the man's short hair white and bounced off the tiny, round glasses perched on the end of his nose. His long fingers danced, streaming over the ivories like soldiers pouring onto the battlefield — and yet, but for the motions of his hands and arms, he sat still as a statue otherwise. He was a ghost from another era in his waistcoat and puffy sleeves, his tie cinched to the throat, his gleaming dress shoes poised over the pedals but never pressing.

God, what would it be like to have those fingers dancing on Jim's skin like that. He swallowed thickly, coughing past the cloud in his neck — and the man glanced up.

The music never stopped, but it paled into insignificance as Jim was struck — full in the face, both barrels, direct hit — by the brightest eyes he'd ever seen. They were grey, so pale as to almost be white, and Jim forgot how to breathe. Who needed to breathe anyway? He was impaled by the stare of an archangel, and suddenly Anthony's religious convictions didn't seem so ridiculous after all.

"Hello," the angel said, *still* playing. Good God, it was impossible. Some bright and jaunty tune, clattering and crashing out of the old piano as though he were trying to shake the dust off by sheer sound alone, and yet he never paused, never looked down, never hesitated.

"Er," Jim gurgled.

"I don't believe we've met?"

God no, Jim would have remembered meeting those eyes before. The way they looked over those little round glasses at him was incredible. He was being studied, scrutinised, examined, calculated — and it turned him on like crazy. One word and he'd strip naked there and then. If the man kept staring, then Jim was going to get hard.

"I'm Oscar and Patricia's music teacher. And you are — ?"

Jim's jaw sagged, but nothing came out.

Thankfully, he was rescued by Oscar, of all people. He came traipsing in, skirting around Jim as though he were part of the furniture, and went to the piano and its heavenly master as if this were all perfectly ordinary. The angel murmured to him and Oscar gave

Jim a blank stare, gaze dropping to his book as quickly as it had risen to look at him.

"That's Uncle James," he said flatly. "Mum says he's moved in because he's fallen on hard times."

The antiquated phrase tripping off Oscar's tongue made the piano teacher chuckle and Jim snorted with laughter. The spell...didn't break, exactly, but loosened its hold.

"Would you introduce us then, Master Lovelace?"

Oscar blinked at the angel, then examined his shoes intently.

"Uncle James, Mr Carr. Mr Carr, Uncle James," he recited, and flushed deeply.

"Excellently done," Mr Carr said and lifted a laughing gaze to Jim. "And pleased to meet you, Mr Lovelace."

"It's Love," Jim said, feeling like a cheesy James Bond caricature and not caring for a minute. "Jim Love."

He'd look as stupid as he had to if it would make the angel laugh once more.

Chapter Three

Jim shamelessly stalked the lessons.

He lounged in the window seat with a book he had no interest in — which was just about every book in the world — and watched over the top of its pages as the angel named Carr played and taught, taught and played. He was relaxed and easy with the kids, music and language flowing out of him as naturally as breathing, and he not only taught the keys but the history of the musicians, the theory behind music — Jim hadn't even known there *was* music theory — and, most tantalisingly of all, he rolled his sleeves up to the elbows to demonstrate a particularly challenging piece. Jim didn't know he had a thing for bare arms but apparently he did.

Despite it, Oscar was silent as the grave, barely speaking to his teacher and plucking out the melodies in torturous hesitance. He plainly knew his basics and could play well enough with two hands, but he seemed slow to obey and slower to enjoy. He was either painfully bored or painfully shy, and was gone as quickly as he'd arrived when the hour was up, but Patricia was chattier — and far more informative.

"Hi, Mr Carr!" she chanted as she stomped in and Jim made a mental note of the name. "Can you tell me more about Mozart, please?"

"Of course."

"Especially the bit where he died."

Dear God, the child was a nutjob.

"Oh, that's not the interesting part," the teacher said, completely unfazed. "Mozart was a prodigy. That's the special part."

"That's boring," she complained, but he managed to steer her on to other music instead of dead people and had her smashing out *Twinkle Twinkle Little Star* in true music lesson tradition before too long. Then he finally looked up.

At Jim.

And *smirked*.

He had a wicked sort of face, despite the sun's magic and his white-blond hair. The smile was broad and genuine for the children, just a happy, harmless man. But there was something else when he smiled at Jim. Something sly that went straight to Jim's dick. He'd taken one look at the angel in a three-piece suit and figured he might like a few lessons of his own — particularly in sin — but the smirk suggested that Jim might be the one needing some pointers after all.

Jim couldn't tell exactly where the sneakiness lay. The smirk lifted at only one side, so perhaps it was his mouth, but there was something about his eyes. Something would change in his eyes, Jim was sure of it. He wondered what those eyes looked like if he was turned on. He wondered if he could play a body like he could play a piano, or whether the teacher became the instrument when the suit was torn away.

God, Jim wanted to know what it looked like when the suit was torn away. If he was that pale all over. If there were signs of fire — tattoos, piercings, scars. If Mr Carr was the devil in an angel's mask or if he was something ethereal that Jim could bring down to earth with a soul-shattering crash. And in all the best places.

He lingered until the end of Patricia's lesson — which seemed to be when she got bored, demanded more details of dying of dysentery or whatever it was that caused dead musicians to be dead and ran off — then slid the book back into place on the shelf and stood up, leaning against the piano as Mr Carr tidied his sheets into a black bag.

"Can I help you, Mr Love?" he asked, glancing up over his glasses again.

Jim's heart skipped a beat and he coughed.

"I was wondering if there might be another lesson going."

Mr Carr raised his eyebrows. They were so fine and fair that they were nearly invisible and Jim only really noticed the motion by the lines that were dug into his forehead. It aged him and yet he looked better for it.

"Only if you have the fee."

"Which is?"

"Rather more than a man on hard times can afford," came the smooth reply, another smirk flashing his way before the pianist stood.

"Don't suppose you do discounts?"

"I don't."

"What about an introductory offer?"

"Afraid not."

"No ten lessons for the price of nine in piano circles, are there?"

"There might be, but not in my case." The bag snapped shut and a pale hand was held out. "It was

27

nice to meet you, Mr Love." His handshake was firm and Jim lingered.

"Jim. Do you come every Friday?"

"Tuesdays, Wednesdays and Fridays."

"Could we make it every other day as well? I could get used to the view."

He hadn't quite meant to jump right over into overt — and bad — flirting, but it didn't seem to damage his cause. The smirk was back. And as wicked as ever.

"There are seats with better views."

"Are there?"

"Oh yes. Ones where the piano doesn't get in the way so much."

"Or the suit?"

It widened.

"Or the suit."

"So what does a guy have to do to get one of those suit-free views?" Jim asked boldly.

"That depends on the man."

"How about a man like me?"

"Hmm." The pianist tapped one of those long, clever fingers against the side of his mouth. Jim wondered what else they could do. "A man living with his relatives because he's fallen on hard times, is plainly musically deaf, but can read Chaucer upside down…"

Heat washed up Jim's neck and into his face.

"That would take a lot of work, Mr Love."

"I don't mind hard work."

"Just as well." The bag was lifted. "I must be going. Lovely to meet you."

"Wait!" Jim said. "Seriously. I'd like to — have a lesson or two from you."

"Somehow, I don't think you mean a piano lesson," Mr Carr said, pausing at the thankfully closed door but not opening it.

"Not really, no."

"Then what kind?"

"What about a different type of finger exercise?"

A snort of laughter broke beyond the façade, then the man's face smoothed out once more.

"I'm not in that kind of business, Mr Love."

"Jim, please."

"Given your question about fingering, are first names appropriate?"

"I said finger *exercises*. You said fingering."

"The point stands."

"Mm, don't think so," Jim said, but yielded. "If anything, the question makes first names more appropriate."

"Let me put it this way, Mr Love."

The glasses were pushed fractionally up that long nose and he paced back to Jim. Leaned in close. The whisper landed hot on Jim's ear and his blood turned to fire in his veins at the words.

"My lessons in fingering are exclusively for those lucky few who earn the opportunity to buy me a drink in a certain bar."

"Name the time and place," Jim said.

"Oh no, Mr Love. I'm not that easy. You have to *earn* that."

Then he was gone. Just like that. Gone in an instant and Jim heard a car engine start and tyres roll across gravel long before he recovered himself enough to even smile.

Christ, that had been —

He shook himself. Sad. That was what it had been. How long had it been since he flirted if just chatting up a random piano teacher had gotten him a semi and a stupid smile on his face? He didn't even know the man.

But then since when had Jim needed to know people? He'd met most of his exes in bars. Shagged a lot more random people in bars, too. Meeting a piano teacher was classy enough on its own and Jim wasn't fussy. If the guy liked to play teacher in the bedroom, too, get out the cane and bend him over a desk, then Jim was totally fine with that. And if he wanted to be ravished and have his heavenly innocence sullied, then Jim would step up to the plate.

Either way, a good shag was good for the system.

And Jim refused to believe that a man who smirked like that wasn't a good shag.

* * * *

Sarah came up to his room when she got home, as though she was his mother and he'd skipped school.

"Did you go job hunting?"

"Did it online," he lied, shrugging. "How was work?"

She shrugged right back, unwinding a floral scarf from around her neck. "The usual."

"Oscar wasn't at school today."

It wasn't the smoothest line that Jim had ever come out with, but then he was out of practice with Sarah. She blinked, then shook her head.

"No, we home-school them both. They have a couple of tutors come up from the village."

"Why?"

"They were struggling with school a bit."

Jim snorted. "No wonder."

"What?"

Shit. He hadn't meant to say that out loud.

"Er. Just meant Oscar's a bit quiet."

Sarah hummed. "He's shy. He'll grow out of it. I hope."

"Think I met one of them. Er. The tutors, that is. Frank Carr?"

"Oh, Francesantonio."

"What?"

"Francesantonio," she replied blithely.

"That's — that's a name?"

Oh, he was definitely the innocence-defiled sort if that was his first name. Christ, he'd probably gone to Sunday school until he was eighteen. And sucked off other choir boys in the confessional while he was at it.

"Well, it's his name," she said primly. "He's an excellent musician. He teaches them piano, oboe and Oscar the violin. They're coming along wonderfully."

Given Oscar's buttoned lip, Jim wanted to suggest paying a therapist instead of a musician but bit that back. He rather liked the musician, after all.

"He seemed nice."

"Yes, he's lovely," Sarah agreed blithely. "Zoe's taking the children to an art gallery tomorrow. Do you want to join them?"

"Er, no thanks."

She pursed her lips. "It would be nice if you'd spend time with them."

"It'd be nice if I looked for work," Jim said flatly.

She hummed again, that same little disapproving tone that Mum used all the time.

"I get it," Jim said. "You want to fix my life for me. Don't. I'll get a job and get out of your hair. I don't need your husband's snide remarks about bringing home blokes."

"What?"

"Your other half. Asked me not to bring home men."

"Well, he just meant…you know, not in front of the children."

"You think I'm going to shag someone in front of the kids?"

"No! I mean they're too young to understand about…that. Men. With men."

"Really," Jim drawled. "Fine. Though frankly that pianist is gorgeous, so it's really Anthony who's been bringing home the blokes, isn't it?"

"Jim!"

"What?"

"Stop being so crude. And cruel! It's just his fa—"

"Right, yeah, it's cruel if I—"

"Stop it! Just stop it!"

The shout was shrill. Downstairs, the murder of the piano suddenly ceased.

"Don't," Sarah snapped. "Just leave well enough alone. Anthony has his faith. Why can't you respect that?"

"Because you won't respect me," Jim returned.

There was a sharp silence. An angry, tense thing, like a string about to snap. The room itself seemed to hold its breath. Then—with a withering look—Sarah turned on her heel and stomped off down the stairs.

Jim didn't join them for dinner that evening.

Chapter Four

"Fine," Jim said, trying to mask his impatience. "Can I leave a copy of my CV anyway? Just in case something comes up."

"Sure," the barista said, holding out a hand. "I'll make sure the manager sees it."

"Thanks."

He had no doubt that it would go straight in the nearest bin, but an application was an application. And he'd signed up for the dole, so he needed to prove he was trying to get work if he wanted his benefit money.

But, frankly, Jim was in a foul mood. He'd spent all morning traipsing around town handing out CVs. He wasn't proud. He'd sweep streets, or serve coffees, or stack shelves. He'd do whatever. A job was a job. And Jim was a lot of things, but workshy wasn't one of them, and the condescending stares of tiny university students as he passed out résumés was getting to him.

Sighing, he stepped back out into the damp and squinted up the road. One more shop, then he'd break for lunch.

The cafe was busy, the windows steaming up from the heat against the rain outside. The music was too loud and the hubbub distracting — and yet something caught Jim's eye and he craned his neck to stare. Out of the dark wood effect, gloomy coats and too-low lighting, there was a flash of white.

He blinked.

It was that pianist.

He was sitting in a corner, a pair of earphones blocking out the universe and those little round glasses nearly falling off the end of his nose. One leg was up, the ankle slung over the opposite knee, and a large sketchpad rested on the resultant frame. He was drawing. And he was left-handed.

Jim had never been jacked by a left-handed guy before.

"What can I get you, sir?"

He shook himself and brushed the thought away. And the barista. Waving a hand, he loped away from the till and tapped the back of the empty chair at the teacher's table.

"Mind if I take this?"

"No, go ahe — hi."

Jim grinned at the surprised look and tapped the chair again. "Fancy some company?"

"Are you stalking me, Mr Love?"

"Would you believe pure coincidence?"

"Not especially," came the waspish reply, yet the little smirk was back. "What brings you here?"

"Job hunting."

"Ah."

"You?"

Mr Carr shrugged. "A hobby to pass the time."

"Drawing?"

"Yes."

"Are you good?"

A white eyebrow lifted. The sardonic arrogance was distractingly attractive.

"I am *very* good," Mr Carr said heavily, as though Jim had personally spat at his mother. "I take it you're not the artistic type?"

"Nope." Jim lounged back, eyeing the long body opposite him. "I can appreciate beauty, though."

"Can you indeed."

"Yup. I like the ethereal aesthetic, myself. Pale colouring, imagery of innocence, that sense that temptation has been resisted thus far but that pressure in *just* the right pla—"

"If you think I am innocent in any sense of the word, then you flatter yourself on your analytical skills."

Jim grinned. "Who says I was talking about you?"

Mr Carr didn't even look up from his sketching. "The state of your jeans."

Jim flushed hotly, shifting to rearrange himself—and stopped.

"You bloody—!"

He laughed. A flash of teeth answered him and those white-grey eyes met his own briefly, something dangerous and mischievous alight in them. It was like looking into fire and wanting to walk forward. Jim laughed again.

"Let's start over," he said and leaned forward, hand outstretched. "Jim."

The sketchbook was briefly balanced against a narrow knee. The hand that met his own was warm and smooth, the grip firm and lingering. The fingers stroked his skin as they fell away.

"Fran."

"Francesantonio, according to Sarah?"

"Mm."

"Are you…Italian?" Jim guessed.

Fran chuckled, his focus back on the paper. "Not precisely."

"Cypriot?"

"Grimsby."

Jim snorted with laughter.

"It's simply an unusual choice of name," Fran continued blithely. "There's no particular reason for it — or at least none I especially feel like sharing."

"Can I earn that, too?"

"Perhaps."

"So, got a boyfriend?"

The smirk flashed up at him. "Do you?"

"Not anymore."

The gaze lingered for a moment and Jim could sense the curiosity.

"Everybody's beautiful," he said flatly and was met with a quiet noise of understanding. "If you're not innocent, you've had one."

"She wasn't my boyfriend."

Jim grinned.

"And she wasn't all that innocent, either. But may I remind you" — the pencil was jabbed aloft, as if referencing God through the cafe ceiling — "Lucifer himself was an angel once."

Definitely a Sunday school devotee, Jim decided.

"So what you're saying is that even angels are demons," he said.

"*Especially* angels. Michael had a flaming sword to lead the armies of heaven. There's not much innocence in a holy war."

"A flaming sword, eh?"

"If *that* is the limit of your pun-making imagination, then you're not going to get very far," Fran interrupted coolly.

"Where do you think I'm trying to go?"

"The inside of my briefs, for one."

"Ooh, a briefs man," Jim quipped. "I prefer boxers myself."

"I'm heavy enough to need the support."

Jim's gaze instantly dropped and Fran chuckled. He was wearing suit trousers again. But his pose hid many virtues and Jim gestured for him to drop the knee.

"No chance," Fran said.

"Why, having difficulty?"

"I'm more afraid that you will."

"You're arrogant and it's hot as hell," Jim said.

"So I've been told."

"Here's what I can't figure out —"

"There's only one thing?"

"Harsh."

"Prove me wrong."

Jim rolled his eyes. Fran smirked. He reached out to pick up his coffee and his throat bobbed. Jim wanted to bite it and had to cough before continuing.

"Here's what I can't figure out. Are you that arrogant all of the time, or do you like to be taken down a peg?"

"Who says those two states are mutually exclusive?"

Jim's dick jumped. Visibly. He had to close his coat again, scowling at Fran's laughter. That was *completely* unfair. Jim had a thing a mile wide for power bottoms, pushy subs, basically anyone who'd bend over but bitch the whole way through that they were infinitely superior to every man alive. He could take or leave literally any of his kinks, but that one sent him gaga.

And by Fran's frigging mindfuck flirting, he *knew* it, too. What a bastard. What a complete and utter bastard.

"If you're seriously asking," Fran murmured, "then if you want to take control of me — even for the, what, two minutes it must take you to finish — "

"Hey!"

"Then you'll have to fight for it."

Jim groaned.

"I hate you right now."

"That's not a bad start," Fran mused.

Whatever he was drawing, it was taking his mind away. His tongue was poking out of the corner of his mouth, a bright pink splash of colour on his otherwise drained face. His eyes were narrowed and his eyebrows tight together, forming a little line between them. Jim wanted to see the picture. And he wanted to suck on Fran's tongue.

"There," Fran murmured and lifted the pencil.

"Can I see?"

"That's the point."

It was torn out and handed over. It was a rough pencil sketch, the telltale lines still there on the bodies to frame their proportions properly. But Jim coughed at the image and his face flooded with heat.

It was a sketch of two men in a public bathroom, one on his knees and the other standing. But the man on his knees had the standing man's hands gripped behind his back, holding him prisoner to the rather obvious blow job that was being delivered.

Jim's mouth itched. His dick swelled slightly. He glanced up to Fran's impassive face, chin propped on his closed fist, watching. Waiting. Looking as though he'd handed over a bill, or an accountancy report, or any myriad of boring things.

"Kneeling will ruin that suit," Jim said hoarsely.

Fran smirked. "I prefer to stand."

"Just as well."

"And judging by the fact you never seem to shut up, you're good with your mouth."

Jim grinned. He was. He said so. He asked if Fran wanted to try it out.

"What do you take me for?" came the complete bald-faced lie of a reply. "I'm not that kind of guy."

"Sure you aren't. You're just sitting here talking dirty to me for a social experiment or something."

"Definitely an experiment," Fran mused, tucking the sketchbook into a bag and draining his coffee mug. He sat back, nursing the dregs, and glanced up at Jim under his eyelashes with a soft smile. "I had a date. But I've got the feeling that I've been stood up."

"Who'd stand you up?"

"A sixty-two percent match, apparently."

"I don't really buy into all that percentages stuff," Jim admitted, folding the sketch and tucking it into his jacket pocket. For safekeeping and all. "Star signs and financial plans and whatever. For me, it's—you know. See a movie, get dinner, have sex. Rinse and repeat. And if you like doing all three things with the same person over and over again, you should be together."

Fran laughed.

Then he cocked his head and said, "Well, I'm not really hungry. So—want to go see a movie?"

Jim stared.

He shouldn't. He had to be on his best behaviour until he could get out of his sister's house and back into his own place. He shouldn't go shagging—much less dating—her kids' piano tutor. Because Jim knew what he was like with a new screw. He'd wear it on his face.

It would be obvious to anyone within a mile of him and he'd want to — and would, given half a chance — fuck Fran in every single room in the house.

Sarah would *kill* him.

But fuck if he wasn't hot. Exactly Jim's type. Bragging about having a big dick in that veiled, cultured manner. Possibility of a left-handed hand job in a cinema. Christ, Jim wanted him.

And Jim's dick had always held more sway over him than his dumb brain.

So a grin flooded his face, even as he knew he should be saying no.

"Yeah," he said. "Why not?"

Chapter Five

Jim couldn't remember a thing about the film.

Not the title, not the genre, not the star, nothing. He could only remember that the screening started at twelve-thirty and the minute the lights dimmed after the deluge of adverts, there was a hand on his thigh.

A warm, smooth, long-fingered hand.

A left hand.

It stayed roughly in that area for about half the film. Roughly, because it started on the outside of his clothes and resting on his thigh and it ended up on the inside and resting around his balls.

But the most maddening part was it didn't do anything else.

Nor did its owner. The whole way through, Jim sat crawling out of his own skin at the hot, heady feeling of fingers around his crown jewels. Every hair was on end. His blood was burning. His nerves were on fire, every breath waiting for something to happen. By the time the credits rolled and the hand smoothly extracted itself as if it had been a perfectly bloody normal place to put a hand, Jim could probably have creamed himself with only thirty seconds of concentration.

"Gents," he grunted instead.

Fran strolled into the toilets like he owned the place. Ice-cool and unruffled. For a moment, even Jim thought he was just going to unzip at a urinal and nothing more — but then he walked into the end cubicle and the closed door wasn't locked.

Jim loitered to perfect his hair in the mirror until the other guy zipped up and walked out, then pushed his way in to join Fran.

Thank God these cubicle doors hit the floor.

Because so did Jim's jeans, the minute he turned the lock over. Fran's hands cupped his balls and drew him out of his underwear as though his junk were delicate — then they dropped away and a single finger stroked up the underside.

And Fran was *right. There.*

Right in Jim's face. Lips grazing his stubble. Eyes closed. Jim swallowed and had to brace his arms against the cubicle walls as Fran leaned his full weight up against Jim's body, slid a knee between his thighs and pushed.

Just pushed up on the balls of his feet.

Gentle. Soft.

Heavy.

Jim caught fire. His whole body went up in flames. The rough rasp of cotton on his aching dick. The single finger stroking the slit, almost painfully sharp. The hot stomach pressed against his own. The grind that was somehow softer than that—a slide?—but twice as erotic.

Fuck-fuck-fuck—

And that breath in his ear. The weight under his own.

Jim closed his eyes and reached. Dropped one hand. Rested it lightly against one firm, perfect, completely fuckable arse-cheek — he could feel it, even if he'd never seen it — and raked in a breath.

He wanted to prove that two-minute remark from the cafe wrong, but…but he'd just sat for an hour and a half with a hand, belonging to the hottest man in the fucking universe, around his balls.

Fuck time limits. He could prove it some other time.

So he squeezed.

Hard.

And thrust.

They slammed together. A shaky gasp sounded in his ear. Fingers scrabbled at his shoulder. A hand cupped him and —

Jim grunted as he came. The world shivered. The tension popped like a bubble and he sighed, sagging back against the door as if he'd never had an orgasm before. Breathed. And clutched, as Fran moved back.

"Fuck that," Jim croaked.

He kicked out of his abandoned jeans and turned, shoving Fran up against the door in his place before tugging up his shirt. His stomach lurched under the wide strokes of Jim's tongue as he cleaned up the mess and Jim just kept right on going. All the way down until he was on his knees in front of Fran's freshly opened trousers, just like the picture.

And facing a heckuva nice bulge in a pair of briefs.

Just like he'd been promised.

Jim nudged the cotton with his nose, tracking the line of an impressive cock and inhaling the heady smell of a man who was incredibly turned on. He wanted to hold on to this moment. Wanted to drag it out. So as the underwear came down, Jim didn't give in to his urge. He kissed the gleaming head, blew lightly on the crop of hair — also white-blond — shielding a heavy pair and licked the crease of hip at each side as he reached up and gripped Fran's wrists in his own.

"Behave," he whispered and drew them behind Fran's back.

And squeezed.

Glancing up, Jim noticed that Fran had tipped his head back against the door. He was breathing heavily and looked a glorious undone mess in his trailing shirt and ruffled hair, cock jutting out as though he were trying to hammer nails into the wall.

And he was in Jim's grasp. Hands imprisoned. And cock about to be.

Jim opened his mouth and sank down.

Careful. Open. Controlled. Jim was a cocksucker in the true meaning of the word — he preferred to fuck, preferred to take command, preferred to be the one exploring and opening and making the bed shake rather than the one who spread his legs and got nailed for king and country, but this was the huge exception. Jim had let only one or two people put anything up his backside, but he would — did, had, would again — suck strangers off in nightclub toilets. Getting to suck Fran off *and* take control? That was sex heaven.

Jim couldn't explain it. He just fucking loved it. The bitter taste that changed from man to man. The heavy weight on his tongue. The stretch of his jaw. The rocking shift in hardness and girth as he rasped his tongue against the vein underneath and Fran's already challenging dick only getting bigger. The razor-sharp focus as Jim opened his throat and raked air through his nose until he could, carefully and with utmost precision, press his nose against Fran's belly and feel his dick halfway down Jim's neck.

Yeah, he could come in two minutes.

But he could deep throat a cock he'd never so much as seen before, too.

He drew off after a few seconds, massaging the shaft with his lips until he reached the head, mentally mapping exactly where Fran's wrists strained against his hands. He was hugely sensitive just below the head and at the very tip, and Jim set to work exploiting it. He didn't need his hands to steady the weight in his mouth. He didn't need to break off for gulps of air like an amateur. And having already come, he wasn't distracted from his task.

Fran let out a muted whimper as Jim sucked in earnest on the head, lips sealed just below it to catch the best nerves. With a grating noise, he silenced himself and Jim glanced up under his eyelashes to see Fran's throat working to keep quiet. His hips strained. His wrists were fighting. But Jim simply swallowed against him when he thrust, resuming sucking when he stopped. Patience. Persistence. Those were the keys. Jim could play a man like a flute and a musician was just begging to have an entire symphony blown from his dick.

The tremor was building.

The erratic twists and attempts at escape were getting weaker but more frequent. Jim sank down one more time — the last time, he was sure — just to feel that power and weight in his mouth and neck and bobbed his throat against the swollen head before drawing back and sucking in earnest. Rapid, hard pulls. The stroking was over and now he was going to jerk Fran off with his mouth better than any hand or arse could ever manage.

And it was the slit that did it.

A single jab from his tongue, mid-suck. A squeeze of his hands.

"Oh God —"

A sharp grunt said it was taking everything Fran had not to come.

"Let me — I'm —"

He tugged his hips back, grinding his arse against his captured hands. And Jim suddenly understood. As the dick in his mouth shivered, Jim didn't pull back like he usually would. He didn't brace.

He sank down.

At the last second, he forced Fran in as far as possible and looked up at the man dissolving above him as he felt the hot, warm flood of release burning down into his stomach.

And only when the softening cock clouded Jim's ability to breathe did he draw off, with one last gentle suck to remember it by.

"F-fuck," Fran stammered and slid. He slid down the door right into Jim's arms and Jim took the opportunity to lick his way into that slack mouth and let Fran taste himself. "Fuck. Fuck."

"In a minute," Jim mumbled.

Fran laughed giddily.

"No. We ought to — go. We should go."

Jim tugged at the somehow still buttoned collar and hauled it aside to find a hot, sweaty slip of neck.

"In a minute," he said.

And buried his teeth there, just to feel Fran squirm.

Chapter Six

"Jim? Jim!"

The banging on his bedroom door woke Jim from a very nice dream involving Fran, a grand piano and a bottle of piano oil. Jim wasn't even sure there was such a thing as piano oil in the real world, but in his fantasy world, it had been a very real and very sexy thing. And had smelled like cherry blossom.

"*Jim!*"

"Wh't!" he yelled through his pillow.

The door banged open and shut again. He squinted one bleary eye up at his sister and groaned.

"S'too early —"

"It's ten past eleven and what the hell is this!" she hissed.

It was the hiss that really roused him from his stupor. If Sarah got mad, she just shouted. He turned over and heaved himself up into a sitting position, rubbing sleep out of his entire face with one hand.

"Answer me!"

"Fucking give me a minute," he grumbled.

"Now!"

Something was dropped in his lap. Small and light. He blinked stupidly down at the folded piece of paper.

"The fuck's this?"

"I was hoping you could tell me. And why Patricia found it in your coat pocket half an hour ago," she seethed.

Blankly, Jim unfolded it. Then winced. Oh.

"She brought it to me in my office. I was on a conference call with a client! Half the staff have seen it! Zoe! Francesantonio! Jennifer! It's *filth*!"

It was Fran's sketch. The blow job that Jim had re-enacted in the cinema toilets. He must have left it in his inside pock —

Wait.

"Hang on," he said. "Why is Patricia going through other people's coats?"

"Don't change the subject!"

"I'm not!" he retorted. "That was in my inside pocket! I didn't leave it on the bloody kitchen table for all the world to see!"

"Well, now my six-year-old *has* seen it!"

"Maybe you should teach her not to go through other people's stuff!"

"Maybe you shouldn't bring pornography into my house!"

Jim burst out laughing. "Porn? It's a fucking dumb sketch!"

"Depicting an obscene —"

"Fuck off, Sarah, I wasn't the one caught shagging my boyfriend in the garage when I was thirteen —"

He ducked the slap and dragged himself out of the other side of the bed.

"Stop being such a fucking judgemental bitch," he snapped as he reached for his jeans. "The kid was asking her piano teacher the other week to go into explicit detail about how Mozart died. A bad drawing" — it was anything but — "of a couple of blokes doing something she won't even understand isn't going to fuck her up worse."

"Don't talk about my daughter like that!" Sarah shouted.

"There's not even a cock in there. They're not even naked," Jim retorted. "You could have told her it was a hug round the middle, whatever, no harm done, but you don't care about that. You care that it's two men."

"That's got nothing to do—"

"It's got everything to do with it. I'm not supposed to bring blokes home — that's what your husband said, but he didn't have an answer when I asked about women. If it had been a bloke eating out a girl, you'd have told her it was fucking *art*."

She swelled like a bullfrog, but Jim's temper was well and truly lost. She sounded like Mum. She sounded just like Mum. And he wanted — viciously, violently — to tell her there was another bi bloke playing the piano in her drawing room right now. He wanted to tell her it was a real depiction of their cinema trip at the weekend. He wanted to tell her Jim had had all nine inches of that incredible dick down his throat and swallowed every last drop.

And the only reason he didn't was he was pretty sure he'd not only out Fran, but get him sacked, too.

So, instead, Jim tore a T-shirt over his head — yesterday's, smelling ripe, didn't care — and shouldered past her onto the landing.

"You can't bring this kind of filth into the house!" she bellowed after him as he stamped down the stairs.

"Surprised you let *me* into the house!" he shouted back, grabbing his molested coat off the hook in the hall. His boots had been scrubbed and polished by some minion or other and he shoved his feet into them savagely.

"Don't you walk out that—"

"I'm not your fucking child!" he roared and slammed the door behind him so hard he heard a picture bounce off the wall and shatter into pieces.

Then he realised he had no way out. The house wasn't even in the village. He'd have to walk for a mile or more just to find a bus.

The piano had stopped.

Fuck it. He'd walk. He zipped his coat against the drizzle and headed for the gates. They'd not open for him, so he scaled the wall, scrambling over the top and dropping into the ditch on the other side. He took the time to thoroughly dirty his boots, spiteful like a little kid, then stuffed his hands in his pockets and stalked off down the single-track lane.

God, he hated his sister sometimes.

He'd forgotten it was there. It was just a little sketch, for God's sake. He'd been a bit busy jerking it to the memory of Fran's cock down his throat that he'd not had the energy to think about a drawing. She could have told Patricia anything, given her any explanation in the world. But no, it had to turn into a blazing row about porn and blokes and the usual bullshit every time Jim's sex life ever popped up as being something that existed and wasn't just about virgin girls in white dresses running through cornfields, or whatever the wholesome Christian movies Sarah probably made the kids watch featured.

She sounded just like Mum.

Jim scowled at the puddles and potholes as he walked. He'd not spoken directly to his mother in nearly two years. Not since his first proper boyfriend. He'd just neglected to mention the thing for men and he'd usually had girlfriends, so nobody had noticed. But, stupid Jim, he'd figured Mum wouldn't mind when he started dating Gabriel. She voted Labour and paid for some girls in Africa to go to school.

Stupid bloody Jim.

It was men, so it was dirty. It was men, so it was filth. It was bum sex and cocks and nasty, nasty porn. That was what Mum thought. That was what Sarah thought. Jim had been near vaginas, too. Near them, on them, in them. Plenty of them. They weren't flowering rosebuds scented with fresh blossoms, either. It was sex, for God's sake. All sweaty writhing and embarrassing noises. It was fun and getting rocks off and fumbling with the condom wrapper. None of it was wholesome.

Why did *his* have to be special?

He sulked for almost two miles, rain trickling down his neck and soaking into his old boots. It was getting heavier and he wasn't really sure what to do about it. He'd left his wallet in his other pair of jeans. His phone was charging on the nightstand. But his pride was battered as all hell and he wasn't exactly going to just walk back in there, cold and wet and miserable. She'd win. And he might be twenty-six, but Jim wasn't old enough to just let her win on that kind of bullshit.

He parked himself in the first bus shelter that he came across, about two hundred gallons of rainwater too late, and stared moodily at the village. They'd all be the same. Big driveways and yawning conservatories. They'd all have the same bogus ideas. Sex through a hole in the sheet to have two or three kids, all with names like Oscar and Patricia — never Ozzy and Pat — and no pets, because pets are dirty. Nobody was going to be having good sex around here.

Except Jim. And he'd done it in a cinema toilet.

God, it'd be satisfying to fuck in every room in Sarah's house. They'd be bound to go away for the summer, right? Maybe he could housesit. Then invite everyone he'd ever fucked over and have an orgy. Or just Fran. Blow him in every room — and maybe fuck him, too, if Fran was amenable. Prove that whole two-minute deal to be bogus.

A car horn blared and Jim sighed, rolling his head back against the plastic frame of the shelter. Great. He'd been out for maybe an hour — no doubt Sarah had come to chew his ear off some more and drag him back home. Or, worse, Anthony. If she'd sent Anthony to talk to him, Jim was going to deck the smug, sanctimonious —

Then he blinked at the car that pulled into the bus stop.

It wasn't the Merc or the BMW. It was a red Ford Focus with a great big scratch on the passenger-side door. And the face that peered at him was very pale, with paler eyes and near-white hair.

Jim blinked, then stepped out of the shelter and got into the empty passenger seat.

"Thanks," he said stupidly.

He'd not expected a Ford Focus. It wasn't what he'd expected a suited and booted piano teacher to drive. He'd expected something cute and artsy — a Mini with a daisy painted on the bonnet or a snug city car with a one-litre engine and a pair of fluffy dice. Instead, it was…ordinary. And the paintwork was grubby. A red Ford Focus, probably the free colour when it had been made and at least eight years old.

"Would have thought you'd drive something higher end than this."

"You have no idea what teachers get paid, do you?" Fran asked in amusement.

"What? You're a teacher?"

"Er, yes? That's why I go to your—sister? Brother?"

"Sister."

"Sister's house."

"Oh, I thought you meant in a proper school."

"I do, but it's the Easter holidays and I supplement my income with the private lessons," Fran said. "We go back next week."

"Still going to be teaching Oscar and Patricia?"

"Oh, yes. But Saturdays." He pointed at the cupholders, where two flasks sat side by side. "Get one of those down, you. You want to talk?"

"No," Jim said grumpily but popped open one of the flasks and downed an obscenely strong mouthful of coffee.

"Want to go back to—"

"Definitely not."

"Okay. Want to just drive around for a bit?"

"Yeah, all right."

The gearstick was stiff. The car lurched as it peeled back out into the deserted road and Jim eyed the village as Fran swung it around and headed not back into the city, but farther out into the country, dropping down into Derbyshire without a word.

"Do you teach music, then?"

"Most of my private clients are for music, yes."

"But not at school?"

"No. French."

Jim snorted. "French? Huh. *Voulez-vous couchez avec moi ce soir?*"

"Yes."

Jim chuckled. "Only bit of French I ever learned."

"Only bit you need. And yes. So will just pulling over in a field somewhere do, or would you prefer to go back to my place?"

Jim blinked at the windscreen, then slowly turned his head to stare at Fran. Fran looked as calm and peaceable as though he'd never said a word. The rain on the windscreen cast patterns on his face, like the water was trickling down his jaw. Like something else could be trickling down his jaw.

Jim wanted to fuck him.

But he kind of wanted to kiss him, too.

"Pull over."

Fran smirked and took a turning off their lonely road. The car bumped and rumbled over a tiny lane and inched into a car park shadowed by trees, completely empty and obviously meant for summer hikers. He coasted it into the far corner, then put the handbrake up and took his seatbelt off.

"Back seat or —"

Jim leaned over and silenced the question. He tangled his fingers into the fair hair at the nape of Fran's neck and pulled until Fran had to either lean over or break something important.

He leaned.

And the shift in angle opened his mouth. He tasted of coffee and spearmint and Jim kissed as though he could drink him. Fran's fingers ghosted at his jaw, then tangled in his hair and pulled, yet oddly gently. A guided persuasion. A call to sink deeper. And Jim sank.

Into the softness of Fran's hair against his fingers. Into the gentle heat of his mouth, like melting into hot springs in winter. Into the rasp of stubble against his own and the tiniest edges of teeth where Fran pushed him, pressed him, asked questions without breaking away.

It was sweet and slow and everything Jim wanted — but nothing like what he needed.

"My sister found your drawing," he croaked, resting his nose against the side of Fran's and keeping his eyes closed. "It has to be filthy, nasty, dirty sex because it's two men together. And she's fucking wrong, so I want something so saccharine it makes a Hallmark movie puke, but right now I feel like I want to punch my way out of my own skin and I need a bit of filthy, nasty dirt."

Fran nudged their faces together, then gently pulled back. He leaned down, arm disappearing between Jim's knees, but before he could comment, the seat groaned and shot back in its holdings until it was as far as it could go. Then Fran — being, quite plainly, a yoga teacher as well as a French-speaking pianist — managed to somehow twist, lift himself over the gearstick and come to rest on Jim's lap, sitting on his haunches with his knees gripping the seat and crushed in either side of Jim's hips.

The kiss should have been soul-sucking filth and yet he cupped Jim's jaw in both hands and it was softer than the one before. For long minutes, they almost lay together in peaceful stillness, lips hugging more than kissing, breathing the same air until it became too cloudy and they would begin again. The coffee taste dulled. The spearmint drifted away. Underneath was simply Fran and Jim would chase the taste some other time, perhaps. In the moment, he simply rested one hand on a thigh, the other at the nape of that slender neck and basked in the heavy warmth that rested all along him, squeezed all together to fit.

Then Fran whispered, "I can't figure you out."

"What?" Jim murmured.

"What do you want? Do you want to be held down and used, like I need an itch to be scratched and who cares if it's you? Like the man who sucked my cock in the cinema toilets like he was born to worship at my feet? Or do you want to bend me over the bonnet and fuck me like a machine and who cares if it hurts?"

Jim swallowed and slowly shook his head.

"Or—"

Fran's lips moved to his ear. Dropped the words slowly.

One.

At.

A.

Time.

"Do you want to fight me all the way down, force me to lose the battle and bite me once you're balls-deep for bad behaviour?"

His cock twitched. His throat dried up.

He nodded stupidly and the little kiss that pecked at his bottom lip before it was drawn in with teeth and softly sucked was both disgustingly erotic and heartbreakingly sweet.

"I know somewhere we can go."

Chapter Seven

Somewhere was a flat.

It was part of a new-ish development. All red brick and no greenery anywhere. Fran had to squeeze the car into a spot, then rummage in the glove compartment for a set of keys.

"This is where you live?"

"No," Fran said. "This is where my brother used to live. He left it to me last year and I'm finally trying to sell it."

Jim sensed dangerous waters and steered well clear.

"Shame," he said. "Bet this place is full of hot French teachers."

"Lot of nurses. Hospital's just down the road. Want to buy it?"

"How much?"

"Hundred and thirty thousand."

"Fuck me."

"On it."

Jim chuckled drily as they ducked through the rain to the communal doors. They were posh flats, that much was instantly apparent. Sleek hardwood floors and real plants in the halls. Fran's inherited flat was on the third floor and the glossy wood hid a heavy fire door that groaned when Fran opened it.

And they stepped into completely naked opulence.

The rooms were enormous. A long, wide hall led off through carved archways into a kitchen and a room probably intended to be the living room. Jim stepped through the arch and admired the bare wood, polished to within an inch of its life, and the grand fireplace that took up half the wall. The windows had nothing to shield them — the racks for the blinds empty — and when Fran flicked on the lights, Jim flicked them back off again.

"People will see."

"And what are you going to be getting up to that you don't want people to see?" Fran asked, grinning in the gloom.

Jim cupped his arse and drew him in for a kiss.

It was open and eager, simultaneously wanton but tame. Fran looped his arms around Jim's neck and he simply laughed when Jim pressed him up against the wall by the mantelpiece and tugged at the buttons on his shirt. It was nice. Normal. Fran's skin was warm and tasted faintly of citrus where Jim kissed it, and he pressed his nose into Fran's armpit and inhaled a heady, erotic scent that he wanted to find more of. In a matter of moments, they were both shirtless and the first flicker of fire came when Jim worked at Fran's belt and was waylaid by a hand in his hair and a sharp yank.

The shove back into the wall knocked the wind from his lungs.

Fran sucked obliviously on his neck, crackles of arousal radiating over Jim like lightning. A knee slid between his legs. Hips were grinding up against his own. Fran was pulling at the button on his jeans and Jim snorted, catching both wrists and returning them to their original position, holding their hands together above their heads.

"Behave," he said, nipping Fran's jaw.

"You're too slow," Fran retorted. He wriggled an arm free and locked it around Jim's neck to kiss him. A foot slid up the wall until the knee was nudging Jim in the ribs. "I can feel you. You want me to blow you? I'll get on my knees and blow you if you want."

He surged. Jim resisted. He held Fran back against the wall firmly and earned himself a giddy laugh.

"Oh," Fran said. "You want to blow me?"

Jim's mouth twitched of its own accord.

"Okay." Both hands came down, catching Jim at the ears. "Go on, then. You were so good last time — tell you what. Get on your knees and suck me off, right here and right now. And if you don't come, I'll ride you. You can just lie back and enjoy. How's that?"

Way too fucking passive, that's how that was. Jim growled, momentarily resisting the push on his head, then yielded. He went down — then caught hold and brought Fran to the floor with him in a tangled mess.

"People will see," he repeated when Fran made to get up. He pushed him up against the wall again, spreading those still trouser-clad legs either side of Jim's hips and trapping his upper body between Jim and the wall, kissing him as if their lives depended on it.

Fran twisted his face to the side with a laugh and squeezed his thighs around Jim's.

"No point in this if you won't get your jeans off," he chided.

"I want to see you first," Jim said, stroking the growing bulge in Fran's suit trousers. "I want to really get a good look this time."

"After," Fran whispered around his tongue and Jim bit him.

"Now."

"Fuck me. Then you can look all you want," Fran said enticingly, breaking the kiss to nuzzle at Jim's neck. He pulled himself up into Jim's lap and Jim pushed him into the wall again to keep him still. "Hey. Come on. Just stay there like that and I'll ride you. Then—"

Jim shook his head, holding him back when he tried to escape again, glancing to either side for ideas. Forget people. *Jim* wanted to see. He wanted to see Fran completely naked and take his time drinking in the sight. He wanted to watch him come undone, not just hear it from overhead. He wanted to hold him down and suck him off without having to concentrate so much and anticipate motion. He wanted to learn how he looked when he came.

He wanted him to stay *still*.

There.

There was a hook nailed into the wall, maybe ten feet from Fran's head. It looked like a curtain hook for the nearby archway, but it also looked solid. And there was another welded into the front of the mantelpiece, plainly for hanging the fire tools.

And Fran hadn't been wearing a waistcoat today. It had been a suit jacket, with braces underneath. Braces that were still dangling empty from his trousers.

Perfect.

Jim used his body weight to force Fran against the wall as he unclipped the braces. Fran laughed, humming happily as Jim sucked on his neck, then started as Jim tied one of the braces around his left wrist.

"What's this?" he asked.

"Told you," Jim said as he tied the other wrist. "I want to see you."

Then he slid aside and tied one of the braces to the fireplace.

It clicked. Fran jerked his arm away, but it was too late and Jim caught the loose brace to stretch it to the other hook. The distance pulled Fran's arms wide and he was stretched out between the hooks, shirtless and on his knees, and utterly exposed once Jim tied it into place.

"You have to be kidding," he said, tugging on the braces. With some effort, he could have just about brought his hands back together.

Jim cupped his chin in one hand and kissed him.

"This okay?" he whispered.

For a split second, Fran's mouth relaxed against his own. A nose nudged his. When he peeked, those pale eyes had closed – and Fran nodded.

Jim kissed him one last time – gentle, grateful – then set to work on his trousers. Arms suspended, it was difficult for Fran to resist him, and soon enough Jim had peeled him out of everything below the waist and sat back to look.

He was –

Gorgeous.

Absolutely fucking gorgeous. He was just – *long.* Long limbs, slender frame, almost delicate-looking. He couldn't have been eleven stone soaking wet. A bruise was flowering on his neck where Jim had bitten him and it screamed for more. His hair was a mess and his glasses—

Jim smirked and removed the glasses. He set them aside on the mantelpiece and brushed a thumb under one exposed, vulnerable eye. Strung out like that, Fran looked as though he'd been prepared for sacrifice.

And he was still squirming. His hands were twisting in the braces. His feet were gathered under him and Jim dragged one ankle out, drawing it over his thigh and using his own body to open Fran's legs. Fran's cock was jutting up, hard as hell and already leaking, and Jim freed his own to join it, watching Fran jolt violently as the heads grazed each other.

"Fuck me," Fran whispered. "God, just hurry up and fuck me, this is mad—"

"I'll gag you."

A minute head shake and Jim filed it away for later. Instead, he reached for their abandoned jackets and pawed through them hopefully. Surely if they'd gotten this far—

Bingo.

Inside pocket of Fran's overcoat. A fresh tube and a foil wrapper.

"You always go prepared?"

"I was hoping to see you," Fran admitted and Jim laughed.

"And here we are," he mused, holding up the wrapper to Fran's lips. "You want this?"

"I'm good without if you are."

Jack swallowed thickly. Really? He could—

He leaned in as he popped open the bottle of lube and smoothed a little onto his fingers.

"You want me to fuck you open, then let you leak all over the floor, is that it?"

"Oh-my-fucking-*God*."

He chuckled and sucked on Fran's earlobe as he reached below. He didn't so much push in as Fran pushed down, then his finger was buried to the knuckle in hot, tight heat.

"Done this before?"

"No, I'm a fucking virgin tied to the stake and you're the dragon, just *get-on-with-it*!"

Jim fisted his free hand in Fran's hair and kissed him. Maybe an actual gag was unacceptable, but tongue and teeth seemed to do just fine. He worked blindly, stealing all the little whimpers and whines until they turned to hoarse groans, until he was deep enough to find that sweet spot, until the first savage jerk battered Fran back against the wall and he gasped so sharply that Jim thought he'd come.

He flexed his fingers and felt Fran do it again.

Maybe he could. Maybe he could be finger-fucked into coming without a hand on his cock. Jim smirked into the messy kiss and tried for it, teasing him again and again until his hand was a mess of lube right up to the wrist and Fran was actively crying, twisting violently in the braces and begging wordlessly around Jim's tongue.

"Can't—can't—*please!*"

Then Jim smoothed a smattering of lube down his cock and shifted forward.

Finally, he let Fran's mouth go. Held his head prisoner by the hair and stared into the pale abyss of a breaking dawn.

And pushed.

Heat. Tightness. A rising howl of completion. Relentless sinking — drowning, drowning, they would both drown — and just when Jim could sink no farther, that incredible jump came again. An electric shock. Fran's entire frame seized and heat crashed onto Jim's stomach.

He saw it.

He saw the exact moment that Fran came. Then, only then, when the fog cleared and Fran sagged boneless in his bonds, did Jim begin to thrust.

It was nasty, filthy dirt.

And it was something else, too.

Chapter Eight

"Incidentally, I don't like bondage."

Jim blinked hazily at the ceiling.

They were tangled together in their abandoned clothes, sticky and messy and quite frankly disgusting. Turned out Fran cuddled. Shamelessly, too. Jim had just lain back and let him and rested a hand on his abused arse in the hopes of a second round later.

It had been fan-fucking-tastic.

Then Fran had said that.

"You—you didn't say."

"No, that was fine. I liked that. But, as a rule, it's not my thing."

Jim sighed in relief and patted the bare bum. "Okay."

A face lifted and nudged at his own.

"Hey," Fran murmured.

"Mm?"

"You feeling better than you were earlier?"

"Yeah," Jim said, sighing like he was breathing out the last of the toxic crap. "That was — amazing. Just the filth I needed."

Fran chuckled. "Sometimes a bit of filth is good for the soul."

He wasn't wrong. Jim wasn't an idiot. This was just sex. All right, so they got along nicely and Fran was all kinds of attractive, but Jim wanted to fuck him. And suck him. And maybe the kissing was very nice indeed, but if it never went further than cum everywhere and enough pulse jumps to cause a cardiac arrest, Jim was fine with that.

Still…

Now he'd thought about it, he sort of wanted a kiss. "C'mere."

Fran shifted up. Jim twisted his face to the side. It was getting stale and tasted of Fran, where Jim hadn't been able to resist eating him out to clean up the mess, but it was also tired and sensual and open. Something in Jim's stomach tugged.

"Do you maybe want to try something less filthy now?" Fran murmured, close enough they could have just dozed off right there and never noticed they weren't in a bed.

"Like what?"

"Like coming home with me and having a proper cuddle?"

"You cuddle even when you've not just had sex?"

"I do."

"Doesn't fit your image."

"And what image is that?"

"Very posh, proper music teacher who probably believes in caning."

"Does that fit with being fucked raw against a wall in my own braces?"

Jim blinked, then chortled with laughter.

"Touché."

"Which brings me back to my original point."

"Eh?"

"I'm not usually one for bondage. Just before you go getting any ideas."

Jim smirked, stroking the naked bum that was still resting in his hand. "Right now, my main idea is pizza."

"Ew."

He lifted his head in shock. *"What?"*

"You can't have pizza. Sex after pizza is grim."

"Huh. Point. You *are* up for a second round, then?"

"Totally selfishly, I want another one of your blow jobs."

"Yeah?"

"Oh my God, yes."

Jim smiled at the ceiling. Well, if that wasn't a boost to his ego.

"Hey."

Fingers tapped his nipple.

"Want to spend the night at my place?"

"I'm allowed?"

"I figure if I let you tie me to a mantelpiece and fuck my brains out, you're probably okay to come back to my place."

Jim huffed a laugh.

"I'll do whatever you want in exchange for the blow job. Within reason."

"That's a dangerous promise with me."

A laugh ghosted over his nipple. "Yeah? You really kinky?"

"Not *really* kinky," Jim objected. "But I have my things."

Slowly, an arm moved over his chest. Then a leg over his hips. Then Fran was sitting astride him, peering down with those unfathomable grey eyes.

"Tell me."

"My kinks?"

"Yes."

Jim twisted his hips and Fran fell off. He caught him up again, squeezing him to Jim's chest, front-to-back.

"Git."

"Guilty."

Fran stopped fighting and relaxed when Jim sucked on his earlobe.

"This will probably get my permission to your place rescinded," he admitted, "but sleepy sex."

"Eh?"

"I have a thing for my partner being really drowsy, or half-asleep."

And damn if that didn't come with consent issues. Jim had only ever been able to do it the once, with Gabriel, after several months together. It was just too much of a minefield otherwise. And it had been the best sex of his entire life, so Jim wasn't pleased about the discovery, to be honest.

"Ahh."

"Not *actually* asleep, but—near as possible."

Fran hummed, stroking Jim's wrist with his fingers.

"And I like blindfolds."

"Wearing them, or someone else wearing them?"

"Both."

"Oh, you might be allowed that one…"

"And, um…okay, this one sounds a bit weird, but hear me out."

"Okay…"

"I've never paid a hooker in my life, but I like to pretend I am."

"That's not that—"

"And in my last relationship, if we went out for dinner or had a takeaway, we had this understanding that if one of us insisted on paying the whole bill, the other would owe them sex. Like. To the point we had to invent a safe word because we couldn't tell if saying no was a real no or playing a fighting game anymore."

Fran nuzzled his cheek, grinning.

"So—hypothetically speaking—if we went back to my place and I just so happened to buy us some Chinese food on the way home, you would be obliged to get down on your knees on my welcome mat and suck me off in return, unless you said—I don't know—pumpkin?"

Jim's tired dick twitched. Fran must have felt it, because he rolled his hips back and chuckled.

"Yep."

"Well, then."

Fran leaned down and kissed him, soft and sweet.

"Fancy some Chinese food and a much more comfortable floor?"

* * * *

They didn't have sex.

Jim distinctly remembered that part. They had Chinese food in the car. Then they collapsed into bed and fell asleep. And he woke up alone with a crick in his neck and sunlight pouring through a gap in a pair of red curtains he'd never seen in his life.

And for a long, long minute, the facts didn't pull together.

They just didn't. Even though he knew he'd gone home with Fran, it didn't click for a minute that he was in Fran's house. And when it did, his first thought was to wonder why he was on his own and not to question the obvious sizzling noise somewhere else and the smell of bacon.

Then his brain came online and he realised he could smell bacon.

"Fran!"

"What!"

"Marry me!"

Laughter.

Jim heaved himself out of the bed. It was old and sagging, yet oddly comfortable. The bedroom was tiny, the bed barely fitting, and when he peeked through the curtains, he was given a view of a row of terraced houses.

So Fran lived in a terraced house.

Jim pondered what he'd find when he left the little red bedroom. It wasn't very personal inside, but he imagined a creative type like Fran would have art all over the walls elsewhere. It'd be classy. Piano in the corner under some fancy homemade throw thing his nana made. Plants everywhere. A cat—he'd be the type of guy to own a posh cat. But he was also a teacher, so this was probably a one-bedroomed starter home, with no back garden and single-glazed windows.

"Jim!"

"What?"

"You want coffee?"

"Please!" he bellowed, then shook himself. Why shout? "Fran!"

"What?"

"Are we alone!"

"Yeah!"

Good. He opened the door and wandered stark-naked out into the hall.

The hall was generous. It was about five feet long. Just enough room for another door—bathroom, he checked—and the top of the stairs. Photos lined the wall space and Jim paused in front of an exceptionally attractive one of Fran in a graduation cap and gown with a woman who was, going by the eyes, his mother.

Christ, Fran looked good dressed up to the nines.

But he looked good dressed down, too, and Jim reached the bottom of the stairs to find there wasn't a hall at all. They simply dropped straight into the kitchen and there stood Fran, bare arse on proud display, a huge bruise where Jim had bitten him the night before, and wearing nothing but a pair of fluffy pink slippers and Jim's T-shirt.

"Hello," Jim said.

"Hi."

"That's mine."

"It is."

"Is any of that mine?" Jim asked, eyeing the bacon sizzling in the pan.

"No."

"What!"

"You still owe me a blowjob. Like hell I'm giving you *more* free food."

Jim laughed ruefully, rubbing the back of his head. "Um, can I rain-check that? Only I'm starving to death and I really, *really* need a shower."

"Shower blow job."

"Deal."

It was—cosy. Companionable. The kitchen was too small to eat in and they took their sandwiches into a tiny living room. It *did* have a little piano, wedged into a corner, though there weren't any fancy throws. The sofa was collapsing, Jim's backside nearly on the floor when he sat down, but the coffee was great and the ginger moggy—not at all posh—was friendly. Probably because they had bacon, but it purred, so Jim didn't really care. Fran slung his legs over Jim's lap and they watched the morning news and made fun of the newsreaders' horribly obvious toupee, then Jim put the empty plate and mug aside and ended up with the rest of Fran in his lap, too.

The blow job was delivered on the sofa, ahead of schedule, and Jim was surprised by a wetroom instead of a conventional bathroom and was allowed to watch that white-blond hair turn a normal blond under the cascade of water, and kiss him in something far better than the rain.

It was just sex.

It *was*.

But it wasn't quite, either, because Jim lingered until Fran could wash all his clothes and hang them on the hot radiators to dry, and they lounged in their towels on the sofa while Fran demonstrated that cats could in fact play fetch and suddenly Jim just unbuttoned his lip and started talking.

"Sometimes I hate my sister."

Fran, sprawled half on the floor and half on the sofa, simply made a questioning noise.

"Sarah. Sometimes I hate her. For marrying Anthony and turning into such a posh bitch. We went to a shit school just like everybody else, but then she went off to university and got posh."

"It happens," Fran said.

"He's a prick."

"Anthony?"

"Yeah."

Fran shrugged. "He pays well. Apart from that, I don't really think much of him."

"Well, there's your facts. He's a prick."

Fran chuckled and levered himself up on one elbow. The towel slipped and bared him to the hip. A hand walked up his own chest and came to rest over his heart, one finger extended to tap the soft beating under his skin.

"Why's he a prick?"

"Because he's too busy bumming Jesus to be a good person."

Fran smirked. "After what we just did, surprised you're resorting to gay sex jokes."

"Yeah, well." Jim shrugged. "Consistency is for dweebs."

"Dweebs? You're not old enough to call someone a dweeb."

"Piss off…"

The smiles faded and Jim swallowed.

"I had this partner."

"Oh?"

"Gabriel. S—he was trans. And, um. He hadn't had anything done yet. He was only like nineteen or something. And he needed stuff doing, you know, only he was broke and so was I—"

"Ah," Fran said softly. "I think I see where this is going."

"So I asked Sarah for help. And Anthony."

"And they said—?"

"No."

Fran hummed, tapping his chest lightly.

"Anthony said it would be wrong and Gabriel needed to get some help. Recommended some — well. Conversion therapists, basically. I never even *told* Gabriel about that part. And Sarah said it was just a fling and she wasn't going to spend like…ten grand on my latest piece. That's how she put it. My piece."

Fran's hand crept higher and tapped Jim's nose. He wrinkled it and earned himself a low chuckle.

"That hurt more," he admitted.

"What, my hand?"

"No, Sarah."

"Oh."

"It hurt more somehow. I could get the religious angle, you know? I kind of…I don't know. Expected it? Wrote him off as a tit and it didn't bother me? But the way Sarah was just so cold about it — it *hurt* Gabriel, you know? He was hurting and I could have helped, and — I did."

"You helped?"

"Yeah. I took out loans and paid for it."

Fran settled his hand by Jim's jaw and stroked a thumb over his stubble lightly.

"We broke up about a year later. Officially, I mean. It had just been sex for a while. But all the money was in my name and he was as broke as I was and…it didn't matter to me, you know? I didn't hate him or anything, we just didn't work out, I didn't want to take it all back. So Sarah got to do this smug told-you-so face and I had all this debt and everything just kind of…collapsed around my ears."

"Is that why you live with them now?"

"Yeah. It's that or the street. And I have to be on my best behaviour — "

Fran snorted with laughter.

"I do!"

"Is that what you call it?"

"I'm not supposed to bring men home. Women's fine, just not men. And she went apeshit because of your picture. And—"

"God forbid you did something really serious, like had sex on the living room floor," Fran quipped.

Jim paused.

"Hey!" Fran snapped his fingers. "I do not need to get fired!"

"They'd never know it was *you.*"

"Only if we didn't get caught."

"Trust me," Jim said. "First opportunity, I'm calling you and we're gonna do it on their rug." He heaved at Fran's knee and pulled him right back up into place for a cuddle. A very close and intimate one, given the dimensions of the tiny sofa.

"Just wank on the rug and tell them it was sex."

"That's not as fun."

"You're not doing it right."

"You've never seen your O-face."

"Nobody calls it that," Fran said very heavily, then laughed as Jim wriggled out and turned over, completely smothering him in man and sofa. "Oh, hello. Up for another one, are you?"

"Maybe. Or, it's nearly lunchtime."

"So?"

"So I'm hungry. And I left my wallet at Sarah's."

"Oh, I *see…*"

"Mm. So could you be persuaded…"

"I don't know," Fran murmured into his mouth, smiling around the sloppy kiss. "I suppose I could brew up an omelette and some salad from the fridge. In exchange."

"For what?"

"You, my desk chair and a bit of your bondage."

"Deal."

Chapter Nine

He'd not been home more than three minutes before he heard the footsteps on the stairs. And heavy ones at that.

"Not today," he said when the shadow fell in his doorway. "I'm not talking about shit today."

"James—"

"No."

He reached out and shut the door in Anthony's face. When Anthony simply reopened it, Jim rolled his eyes and pushed past him into the bathroom, locking that door.

To hell with it. He could do with another shower anyway. The smell of Fran's shampoo in his hair was just distracting.

He was certain Anthony didn't know that Fran was queer as a cauliflower quail. And the gross temptation to rub Anthony's face in it, in one of those dreaded bisexual creatures teaching his kids, was powerful. But it would be an unforgivable breach and the best way of dealing with it—and retaining any sanity in this household he might be allowed to keep—was to just avoid Anthony altogether.

And going out for sex with Fran at all hours was definitely going to help.

He showered leisurely and took his time perfecting his hair in the mirror once he was done. By the time he came out, Anthony had disappeared and Jim was left in peace to change and lounge on the bed, half-heartedly raking through job adverts online.

Until the next knock.

"Fuck's sake," he muttered. "What!"

"It's just me."

Sarah. Great. He'd have been more receptive to Patricia, frankly.

"Can you bugger off?" he shouted. "Trying to apply for a job here."

She ignored him and opened the door anyway. He grunted.

"I'm sorry about earlier."

"No, you're not."

"Well, no, I'm sorry for shouting," she said.

"Whatever."

"Jim…"

He sounded like a surly seven-year-old, but he didn't particularly care. Her kid had gone through his stuff and half of Sarah's pissiness was because the picture had shown two guys. God forbid she found his porn collection. God forbid she found out he *had* a porn collection.

"I actually wanted to talk to you about something else," she said, perching on the end of the bed. He eyed her with distaste and deliberately didn't move his feet to offer her more room. "You know we take the kids away on holiday every May."

He grunted.

"Well, usually Zoe housesits for us, but —"

His ears pricked up at that. Housesitting? As in, alone? In the house? For their three-week cruise in the Bahamas or whatever the fuck it was this time?

" — family in Rouens —"

Alone. Blissfully alone. No shouting matches over sketches of blokes doing perfectly normal things. Oh hell, fuck normal. He could do perfectly *ab*normal things. All over the house if he wanted!

" — hoping you would —"

He could watch porn from Anthony's prized armchair. He could wank in the shower. Oh, Christ, he really could get Fran to come over and have sex in every room in the place. Hole in the sheet sex and kinky sex and really fucking weird sex. Sex by the windows and in the cars and, if the weather was good, sex on the goddamn driveway. Gravel rash! He'd never had gravel rash before.

"Jim?"

He blinked.

"Sorry. Zoned out. Er. You want me to housesit?"

"Would you?"

"When?"

"The last three weeks in May."

That was only a week away. Three weeks. Three weeks of absolute heavenly bliss stretched out in front of him. Jim hadn't felt so euphoric since he'd walked out of prison.

"Sure."

"Really?"

"Yeah. Sure. No problem. I can do that."

"Thank you," she said, flashing him a little smile. "It's such a struggle to know who to ask when Zoe's not available. Can't trust anyone these days, not with the safes…"

"It's fine," Jim said, grinning. "That's what family is for, right?"

"Oh, and I wanted to ask you something else."

"What?"

"Well—Oscar."

He frowned. "What about Oscar?"

"Has he, um. Has he said anything to you?"

"About what?"

"I don't know. Anything, really."

"Nope. Didn't know he *could* talk," Jim joked, but it fell flat.

Sarah frowned. "He's always been a bit quiet, but he's been acting downright miserable lately. I'm getting a bit worried, but he insists he's fine. Could you maybe have a word with him? Anthony doesn't really see too much of the children, what with the parish, and maybe Oscar will talk to a man before his mum. You know. Might be a boy thing."

Jim privately doubted it. The kid was only ten and he was a skinny little rake of a ten-year-old at that. He'd probably not figured out *he* was a boy, never mind what a girl was.

But in light of Sarah's heaven-sent request, he just shrugged.

"Yeah, okay. I doubt he'll want to talk to me, but I'll ask," he said, then made a shooing motion. "Now go on. I have to finish this application."

"Good luck!"

The minute she shut the door, he plonked the laptop on the side and reached for his phone.

Me: You busy in May?

Fran: What, the whole of May?

Me: Pretty much.

Fran: Yeah, it's called a job. Try one, you might like it.

Me: Cheeky shit. APART from work.

Fran: I don't know. Not really I guess. A whole month is a bit broad.

Me: I'm going to be housesitting for Anthony and Sarah.

Me: And I have ideas.

He counted in his head. Thirteen rooms in the house if he included the garage.

Me: Thirteen ideas. Plus one for outside.

Fran: I'm listening…

* * * *

Despite his ideas, Jim didn't see Fran again until Saturday, when he followed the sound of piano music to find Fran and Oscar in the middle of a lesson. Jim sat in the corner with a book — the right way up, this time — and watched not Fran but Oscar.

And he hated to admit it, but Sarah was right.

Jim couldn't ever remember Oscar being a chatty or sociable kid, but he was picking at the piano as if he wanted to disappear through the floor. He cringed away when Fran talked to him, even though Fran's voice was low and musical and little more than a murmur in the soft quiet of the room. His head was firmly down and he had to be coaxed to even look up at the sheets.

He looked bloody miserable.

And Jim frowned at the back of his head, wondering why. He didn't go to school, so he wasn't being bullied. His tutors all seemed decent enough from what Jim had seen. Even the little wacko Patricia left him alone him — she'd been busy beheading her boiled eggs that morning and had ignored Oscar's presence completely. And if he was lonely, why would he hide away from Fran like that instead of trying to squeeze more time with him?

There was definitely something up.

As the lesson closed and Oscar scurried out of the room as if he were being chased, Jim cleared his throat.

"Fran?"

"Patricia's lesson is next, Jim."

"Yeah, I know. But it's a quick question. A serious one."

That earned some attention. White-grey eyes flashed over the top of those tiny glasses. They held Jim's stare and for a beat, he forgot how to breathe, before the shrill twittering of some fighting birds on the lawn outside disturbed the silence.

"Oscar."

"What about him?"

"Has he — said anything to you?"

"Such as?"

"He seems kind of miserable. Any ideas?"

There was a long pause. Fran opened his mouth, then closed it again. His gaze slid sideways to the window and he licked his bottom lip, frowning slightly.

"I—"

The drawing room door banged and Patricia bounced in with her music book. She launched herself at the piano stool, hauling herself into place, and held out what looked like a mashed fairy cake to Fran.

"Oh, thank you, Patricia!"

"It's a butterfly. See?" She pointed at the middle.

"I see a caterpillar. Butterflies have wings."

"I pulled them off."

There was a short pause. Jim snorted with laughter and got up, sliding the book back into place on the shelf. He hadn't read a word anyway.

"I'll come back in a couple of hours," he said. "Good luck."

"Uncle Jim! There's one in the kitchen for you, too!"

"Thanks, flower!" he yelled over his shoulder — and studiously avoided the kitchen and whatever fresh hell had been unleashed inside.

He stayed in the safety of his room, pretending to look for job adverts but in reality scrolling through Grindr and wondering if he would find Fran on there somewhere. When the dulcet tones of Patricia doing her level best to destroy the piano tapered off into blissful, beautiful silence, Jim heaved himself back off his bed and headed downstairs, ducking into the drawing room just in time to see Fran rising from the stool.

"Don't get up on my account." He grinned.

An eyebrow rose coolly.

"How can I help you, Mr Love?"

"Oh, *Mr* Love, is it?" He smirked but then dropped the act and perched on the window seat. "Oscar. You were going to say something."

Fran pursed his lips. "Something I'd rather not say where it could be overheard." By Oscar or by someone else, he left hanging.

"All right," Jim said. "Could I ask for a lift into town?"

"Into town?"

"Yeah. Sort of Woodseats area. Near the police station. Do you know it?"

A smirk flitted across Fran's face. "Vaguely," he said. "All right."

Jim shoved his hands in his pockets and followed him out to the car, pausing only long enough for shoes and keys. He had zero intention of going anywhere but a little house in said area, with a red bedroom and stairs that came up out of the kitchen, and by Fran's comment, they both knew it.

Still, it didn't derail the conversation, because the minute that the gates closed behind Fran's car, he started to talk.

"You don't tell Oscar that I told you this, all right?"

"Of course."

"I've been teaching him about six months and he's been getting steadily quieter and more difficult to reach."

"He's acting up?"

"The opposite. He does exactly as he's told, no more and no less, answers in monosyllables and takes off the split second he's allowed. And yet he enjoys the piano. He's always enjoyed it. So I've been keeping an eye out and I meant to raise it with Anthony, but — well — "

He stopped. Jim waited as they navigated a tricky junction, then made a questioning noise.

"The other day he was asking about famous women musicians."

Jim raised his eyebrows. "So?"

"So I told him some. Said I'd bring some of their work, too, and he could try out that. Then he asked if I knew anything by a woman musician who used to be a man."

Jim heard it. And for a moment, it just washed past his ears without clicking into place, as though Fran had started speaking his French. Then it crashed together into sense and his jaw dropped.

"Oh."

Fran hummed.

"You think he's—"

"I've no idea," Fran said peaceably. "I said I didn't, but I'm sure there's some, and I'd find out."

"Did you?"

"It was only last week. With school back in session, I've not had a chance, and—no offence, but I didn't want to remark on it today with you in the room."

"Yeah, I get it," Jim murmured absently, his brain working overtime. Oscar wanted to know about trans women musicians. And Jim didn't know of many ten-year-old boys asking those kinds of questions who weren't working something out in their heads.

And in that household, where would Oscar have picked up that trans women even existed? He had a habit of reading his dad's newspaper at the breakfast table on Sunday mornings, so unless there'd been an op-ed, Jim couldn't imagine it coming up. Anthony flatly refused to talk about that sort of thing. And Jim didn't really know anything about trans people beyond his crash course from Gabriel a few years ago, but he remembered the shitty newspaper headlines and the rule about avoiding the comments section, and he couldn't imagine it had got any better.

Shit. Shit, if Oscar was working out something like that in his own head and he only had the *Daily Telegraph* as a guideline —

"That silence had better be you working out how to support him," Fran said tightly and Jim jumped.

"Crap. Yes. Yes, it is. You know it is."

"I don't."

"Well, it is," Jim retorted. "Shit." He raked both hands through his hair. "That's — I don't think I need to tell you that's not a great family to be figuring out that kind of shit in."

"I don't know *what* he's figuring out," Fran said. "For all I know, there's a child at one of his clubs that's trans. He might have a crush on them. He might be gay and have confused it for being a girl. Certainly I had a few thoughts like that when I first realised I liked boys, that it must mean I was a girl."

"Please tell me you were, like, ten, because I certainly didn't."

"I was about seven. Seven-year-olds aren't known for their incredible reasoning skills," Fran replied airily.

Jim snorted. "That's true. But — even if it is just that, if he's got a crush or he's gay or whatever, Anthony still isn't going to like it."

"He'll have to learn to like it," Fran said. "After all, he has three kids. There's fairly decent odds one of them's going to turn out queer. And he's already got a bisexual brother-in-law so —"

He shrugged. Jim chewed on his lip thoughtfully, staring blankly out of the glass as they peeled up past the police station and turned off into the housing estate where Fran's home nestled.

"I only knew Gabriel. I'm not exactly a trans dictionary."

Fran made a so-so gesture with his hand. "I know a bit. I questioned for a while myself."

Jim blinked. "You did?"

"Mm."

"You don't look—" Jim started, then groaned. "Aaaand I walked right into that dumb remark."

"You did."

"What's the punishment?"

"You can blow me."

"That's a punish—"

"In the bathroom."

Oh *man*, those tiles would hurt the knees. But Jim nodded. Fair price.

"Okay. Er." He glanced at those long legs as they worked the pedals, the little car shimmying into a little space. "You mind if I ask?"

"Not really. It was a few years ago."

Jim held the question under his tongue until they were inside and the front door closed, then it spilled out. "Is that why your name is a bit...out there?"

Fran snorted with laughter. "Usually I would bite your head off for that, but you're actually right. I used to have a really boring name."

"Like Jim?"

His lips twitched. "*Exactly* like Jim, actually."

"Oh my God, you're kidding."

"Nope."

"Jimmy Carr!"

Fran cracked up laughing. The sun blazed out of his merriment and Jim couldn't help but catch him round the hips and drag him in for a cheeky bite of the neck.

"Oi! Philanderer."

"And proud. So you chose a new name?"

"Yeah, in university."

"Why?"

"It was a period of exploration and I felt…unsettled with the name I had. With the person I was. I knew a couple of friends at the uni LGBT society who were trans and some of what they said struck a chord, in an odd way."

"So…you're trans? Non-binary?"

Fran shrugged as he worked his tie off. "I suppose the latter."

"You suppose?"

"I never completely worked it out. I supposed the closest I ever got was agender, but here it is—I have absolutely no idea what anybody *means* when they say they are a man or a woman. Cis or trans. I don't know how people know that."

Jim frowned, cocking his head. "Eh?"

"I don't know what they mean. I can't understand what it is people are feeling, understanding, *knowing*, when they say they are one gender or another. I know I was assigned male because the requisite parts are present and accounted for and I've seen my paperwork. But I can't seem to grasp what it is that being a man is supposed to feel like. It feels like asking me to understand what it's like to have six arms. It isn't something I can imagine."

"Okay…"

"I can understand that sense of being distressed by something being wrong, so I can sympathise with dysphoria and understand the need to rectify it. I have a couple of mild issues that could be a gender identity issue, I suppose, but even there I'm not entirely sure. But I don't know how those people know they are something else, rather than simply not."

"I don't get it," Jim said blankly. "If you just don't get gender, aren't you like me? Cis? I mean, I know I'm a dude because I have the bits and I'm cool with that."

"I'm not a hundred percent cool with that."

"Oh. *Oh.*"

Fran shrugged as he stripped out of his waistcoat.

"So, if I can ask…"

"I wasn't at ease with a heavily masculine name. I was like you, I was Jim. Ironically, people in my French classes called me Jamie and that was much better. But I was usually Jim. And it felt—uncomfortable. The person they were seeing wasn't actually me. And when I swapped it out for Fran, it was a much better fit and the problem went away."

Jim nodded slowly. "But—is that a gender thing? Or just a crap name? I mean, might…I don't know, might Elijah work better?"

"Elijah?"

"I don't know, making it up!"

Fran laughed. "Maybe. I don't know. It wasn't the only thing. I had—have, still, really—an issue with…uh…certain sex acts, I suppose."

Jim coughed. "Er."

Fran went pink.

"Certain sex acts?"

"Yes."

"Like?"

"I—"

"…Fran?"

Fran heaved a deep sigh, rolling his head back. He cupped his neck in both hands and began to massage it. "I don't like to fuck is the best way of putting it."

"Er—"

"I mean, use my cock for that purpose. To penetrate. It feels oddly like it's not a part of me when I do." He waved a hand. "I don't really know how else to explain it. I don't like to do it and it feels like it's something deeper than…than the way I don't like bondage."

"So we—"

"I've not fucked you."

"I've sucked you off, though."

Fran smirked. "Yes, well, I don't get the same issue with that, for some reason. Not with you, anyhow."

"Not with me?"

"It's hard to explain. You touch me elsewhere. I've been blown before and it's been a hands-in-lap scenario for my partner. That wasn't great. Same sort of problem. But you tend to hold my arse or finger me or rub my legs and so it's fine."

"'Fine'."

"Oh, shut up. You know what it is."

Jim flashed a grin but shifted uneasily on his feet. "It *is*, though? You didn't say it—"

"There wasn't an issue. I promise. I like the blow jobs, trust me."

"Well. Yeah. Good. If—if there's an issue—"

"You know what you need to know," Fran said gently. "Don't go second-guessing what we've done because of this. It's mostly ancient history."

"Is it?" Jim asked doubtfully. "How? It's part of you."

"It's not a part that causes me issues anymore," Fran said. "I told you, I was questioning. Exploring. I was—I was at a stage in my life where I needed all the answers. You know how when you work out you're queer, sometimes you feel that need to be able to pin a label on all of it, to break it down into every component part and really know, really understand, every single aspect of who you are because of it?"

"I guess…"

"That was me. I was in those circles where it had to matter, it had to *mean* something. I had these issues with my name, with my penis, where I wasn't quite like other men. But I wasn't a woman, and when my friends—and they weren't being spiteful, they were trying to help—but when they would probe and ask, pick away at my thoughts with me, I started to realise I didn't even understand what they meant when they said gender."

"That whole thing about six arms?" Jim asked.

"Yeah. My thoughts stopped at my sex. I was male. That much was obvious. Beyond that, I couldn't understand what they were getting at. There was something off that meant I wasn't exactly cisgender, but if I didn't even understand what a gender was supposed to feel like, how could I have one?"

It clicked.

"That was your answer," Jim said.

"The nearest I got, yes."

"So you're—genderless?"

Fran shrugged. "Agender, maybe. To be honest, after I graduated, it mattered less and less to me. I don't think I ever really found the answer, but I also stopped asking the question. I had a new name. I don't have a problem with people knowing what's in my briefs. As long as I don't do certain sex acts, I'm fine. So these days I tend to just say I'm a man and leave it there. I suppose…I stopped feeling the need to know."

"That's a pretty weird statement for a teacher," Jim said seriously and Fran smirked.

"Yeah, well, don't tell my students that not every question needs to be answered."

"You'd get sacked."

"Oh no, long as I said it in *French...*"

Jim grinned, reached out and stroked a hand down slim ribs. Fran leaned in the living room doorway and watched him through curious eyes. Jim wanted to touch. Do something sweet. Not just for Fran giving him what he needed to maybe help Oscar, but also for the little slip of something vulnerable under the veneer. The trust. The opening up.

God, Jim was in a bit deeper than he'd thought.

And like he usually did when he sank too deep, Jim resorted to humour to stay afloat.

"Why the name? You just want to fuck with university forms and their short boxes or what?"

Fran sniggered. "You'll laugh."

"Yeah?"

"It was a drunk joke at four in the morning."

"Fucking hell, *really?*"

"Mm."

Jack grinned. "Oh, come on. Tell me."

"A mate—I think it was Kelly, actually, I'm not entirely sure now—but a mate was saying if I couldn't decide if I was a man or a woman then my name should be some mixed-up mindfuck. And we went searching online for names and we found Francesantonio. Frances is a girl. Antonio is a boy. Boom."

Jack rocked with laughter and was steadied when a warm body slid up against his and shored him up. He grinned against the fleeting kiss.

"Mindfuck. That's definitely you."

"Mm. It just sort of stuck."

"*You* just sort of stick. I kind of like it."

"I figured," Fran murmured, nudging their noses together. "Want to get something to loosen me up?"

Jim ghosted his knuckles down the back of pristine cotton.

"I still owe you that blow job."

"Ooh, true."

"Then something to loosen you up?"

Fran smirked and bit his lower lip before slowly letting go and—even more slowly, reeking of sex appeal better than a professional porn star—walking backward up the stairs.

"Only if you're good," he said and Jim beamed.

"Best behaviour. Promise."

Chapter Ten

Jim couldn't decide whether to wait or not.

It would just be a few days before they all buggered off to Trinidad or wherever the fuck—Jim hadn't been listening, he had no idea, really—and part of him wanted to just let things lie until they got back. It would be easier for everyone. But then the other part of him, the part that remembered what it was like to be closeted because he was afraid of losing everything rather than because he just didn't want nosy parkers in his business all the time, grated against the idea of letting Oscar sit worrying about it for any longer.

If that was, indeed, what he was worrying about.

With Anthony for a father, Jim kind of hoped Oscar was straight as a die, one hundred per cent a boy, and was just worried about a friend from his riding club or something.

God, Jim hoped it was that.

Still, it niggled away at him for the next couple of days and in the end, Jim decided to act sooner rather than later. If the kid was worrying about himself, he could at least go on his holidays knowing his uncle had his back. And if it was all about some mate of his, then he could go knowing he could talk to Jim about it if he needed to. Even if Jim wasn't so shit-hot at the whole agony-uncle thing.

He left it until after dinner on Thursday, when Oscar usually vanished into his room and Patricia would be busy winding Aggie up into a frenzy to torment Zoe or her mum. When he heard the first shouted, "Patricia, for God's sake!" he knew they were safe from being interrupted and abandoned his laptop for Oscar's room.

Oscar's bedroom door was open, but Jim knocked anyway. He'd never been into any of the kids' rooms and he'd expected...well, he'd expected it to look like a kid's room. But it was the same lacey night terror of his own room and the only hint that anybody lived there at all was a pair of socks sticking out of the top of a hamper and a thick book on the nightstand. Another was clutched in Oscar's hands and he blinked owlishly over it.

His eyes were pink around the edges, too. He'd been crying.

But Jim barely knew the brat, when it came down to it. He hadn't visited much before this whole fiasco had started, hadn't been to his mum's and seen them at birthdays and Christmases for years, and Sarah sure as hell hadn't been bringing the kids into the shit part of Sheffield to visit him in his grungy flat. What was he supposed to say? *Hi, your piano teacher who I'm shagging thinks you might be bent as a bumper car, want to talk about it?* That'd go down a treat.

So he went for a line as boring as his brother-in-law.

"What you reading?"

The wide-eyed stare dropped.

"Just a book."

Jim sat down on the end of the bed and squinted at the title.

"*Around the World in 80 Days?*"

"Yeah. It's good."

"It's a bit advanced for you, isn't it?"

"It's good," Oscar repeated flatly.

"Okay. Whatever floats your boat," Jim said, shrugging. "Hey, uh. Is everything okay?"

Oscar stiffened.

"Fr—Mr Carr said you're not yourself lately," Jim continued awkwardly. "Said you were asking some…questions."

"No."

"Said you were asking about—"

"I wasn't."

Jim paused. Oscar's knuckles were going white around the edges of the book and he was shaking his head.

"Hey. Kid. It's okay."

"S'not—"

Oscar glanced toward the door. Jim raised his eyebrows, then got up and closed it. Then feeling like a little kid—feeling like he used to, when it was just him and Sarah hiding in her room while Mum and Dad bawled out their impending divorce downstairs at a volume that would rival a rock concert—sat back down and held out his fist, little finger extended.

"Promise I won't tell."

"Only girls pinkie promise," Oscar mumbled, going scarlet.

"Bollocks," Jim replied. "I make pinkie promises all the time and I'm a twenty-six-year-old man. Come on, don't leave me hanging."

There was a short pause. Then Oscar put down the book and locked his little finger into Jim's.

"Promise I won't tell a soul," Jim said and squeezed before letting go. "So you going to fill me in?"

Oscar shrugged, picking at the duvet.

"Mr Carr said you were asking about classical musicians who were women."

A tiny nod.

"Especially ones that used to be men."

Shoulders came up. Oscar shrank down into the duvet, pulling it right up over his head. Jim sighed and kicked up his feet, stretching out over the sheets beside the now-hidden lump.

"I bet there were," he told the ceiling.

The lump didn't move or make a sound.

"Did your mum ever mention Gabriel to you?"

There was no reply, so he shrugged and carried on.

"He used to be my boyfriend. And before he used to be my boyfriend, he used to be someone else's girlfriend."

He didn't mention that Gabriel would have castrated him for putting it like that. They could have that chat some other time. And anyway, it worked. Slowly, the lump migrated until it was under Jim's armpit. He dropped his arm over it in a loose hug and carried on.

"There's always been people like that. You know how they tell if a baby is a boy or a girl? They just look. If it looks more like a girl, then it's a girl. That's what they say. Only none of us look like babies when we're all grown up, do we? Things change. So sometimes they get it wrong. They said I was a boy when I was born and they were right. They said Gabriel was a girl and they were wrong."

The lump wriggled. A tiny voice emerged.

"What was Gabriel's name?"

"Before? Oh, I can't say."

"Why?"

"I didn't know it," Jim confessed. "And he didn't like people asking."

Silence.

Jim licked his lips and took the plunge.

"Oscar's a bit of a boring boy's name," he said. "I bet there's some great girls' names, though. Much better than Oscar."

Slowly, fingers emerged and pulled the duvet down. Wide brown eyes stared up at him, ringed in red. Oscar's face was a mess of tears and snot, but Jim didn't have the heart to tell him to blow his nose. He looked the dictionary definition of utterly miserable—but there was a tiny note of something brighter when he spoke.

"Can't decide."

"What girls' names do you like?"

Oscar shrugged and Jim ruffled his hair.

"C'mon," he said. "This is what uncles are for. Risk-free running of ideas."

"Promise you won't tell anyone?"

"Pinkie promised, didn't I?"

Slowly, Oscar wriggled back out, sitting up beside Jim but still firmly under his armpit.

"Um. I like—I like Charlotte. And…and Rebecca. And Juliet…"

Piece by piece, the little list inched out. And name by name, Oscar relaxed. The tears dried up and—

unfortunately, all over his face—so did the snot. But he stopped picking at the duvet so much and stopped looking as though someone had drowned his kitten. And when Jim steered him firmly away from Lucy on the grounds that his first girlfriend had been a Lucy and a complete lunatic to boot, he even managed to wring a little laugh out of the brat.

Until the knock on the door.

"Oscar?"

He froze up under Jim's arm as the door cracked open. Sarah blinked at them through the gap, frowning.

"What's the matter?" she asked and her eyes narrowed. "Have you been crying? Jim, what's—"

Jim raised his eyebrows and made an exaggerated throat-cutting motion. "Man-to-man talk here, Sarah."

"Man-to-man—"

"Girls," Jim said heavily.

Oscar cringed. But Sarah's face brightened like a dawning sun.

"Oh!" she said and positively beamed. "Oh, I *see.* Well, I'll leave you boys to it, shall I? Lights out in half an hour, though, please, Oscar!"

"Yes, Mum."

The door snapped shut again and Jim waited until he heard her footsteps pass into Patricia's room.

"Hey." He squeezed the rigid shoulders. "I won't tell her. I'll just let her think you've discovered a pretty girl at your riding lessons or something, yeah?"

Oscar paled. "Um."

"Oh, you have?"

"No."

"You have," Jim said decidedly. "What's her name?"

"I haven't."

"Name."

"Hannah. And it's not riding lessons."

There was a long, long pause.

Then Oscar squeaked, "She goes to swimming club," and vanished back under the duvet.

Jim chuckled. "Good—" He paused, then poked until he found the side of Oscar's head and leaned down. "Good girl," he whispered.

A little hand squeezed his arm through the covers.

"I won't breathe a word," he said. "Promise. But give us your hand. I want to make another promise."

It emerged and Jim wound their little fingers together again.

"I promise," he whispered, "that no matter what you decide—if you're Oscar, if you're Charlotte or Juliet, or even if you're Lucy—I'll have your back, all right? Still your uncle."

The hand unlocked and squeezed his own tightly. A muted sniffle reached him and he ruffled the duvet roughly where Oscar's hair was hiding.

"Get yourself off to sleep," he said. "And when you want to talk, you know where I am."

He escaped at about the same time that Sarah came back out of Patricia's room, looking as frustrated as she usually did when dealing with the middle monster. But her face brightened and she gestured to Oscar's closed door with a smile.

"He's at that age," Jim said with a shrug. "Needed a man to talk to."

"Good talk?"

"Oh yeah," Jim said, then stuck his hands in his pockets. "In light of my awesome uncle skills, mind if I borrow the car? Got an errand to run."

She sighed—but then tipped her head to the side and smiled.

"Go on, then," she said. "Just this once."

Jim grinned and loped off downstairs. He hadn't even made it out into the rain before he sent the text.

Me: Want some lowbrow sex in the back of a posh car? I got the Merc and a box of fancy condoms ;)

Fran: Deal

Me: Plus we need to talk

Fran: No deal.

Me: Tough ;)

* * * *

Afterward — with the Merc on Fran's street, the back seat needing a valet's attention and the guilty parties wound up together on Fran's sagging sofa watching some shit late-night sitcom on the telly, Jim finally gathered a couple of brain cells together and remembered that he'd wanted to talk.

"You were right."

"I'm always right," Fran replied serenely, then shifted to look up. "About what?"

"Not *always*."

"Yes, always."

"You can't be."

"Name a time when I was wrong."

Jim thought about it.

"Bondage."

"I'm right about—"

"You said you never like it, and you liked it at that flat."

Fran snorted. "Fine. One time. That's an anomaly. It's not statistically significant."

"Good God, put your degree away for five minutes—"

"That's *school*, you oik. Nowhere in a French degree did we talk stats."

Jim found an ear and bit it. Fran snorted with laughter but shrugged him off.

"Anyway," he said. "What was I right about this time?"

"Oscar."

The smirk slid away. "Oh?"

"He, uh. Christ. She?"

"She?" Fran echoed, then blinked. *"Oh."*

"Yeah. Don't let him know I told you. I promised I'd not tell anyone and I'm only going to tell you because you picked up on it."

"'Course not. But—she? Really?"

"Yep."

Fran winced. "That…that might be complicated."

"Yeah. Anthony's going to go spare."

"*Sarah's* going to go spare."

"Yeah, but it's Anthony who'll try and send him—her—fuck, I don't know…"

"Did…" Fran paused. "Christ. Did they mention pronouns?"

"I don't think it had occurred yet. They've thought of names, though."

Fran pushed himself up and twisted around so they were side-by-side instead of sprawled all over each other. His hair was getting overly long and he shoved the fringe back. Jim rather liked it.

"I didn't think coming out could go worse than mine, but I've a feeling theirs might."

Jim raised his eyebrows. "You had a crap coming out?"

"Yep."

"What happened?"

There was a long pause.

"Sorry," Jim said. "Forget it. I—"

"My dad hanged himself."

Jim dropped his brew. "Fuck!"

Thankfully the tea had cooled to tepid, so Fran simply vanished and came back with a damp cloth. They cleaned in silence, then Jim sat back and patted his lap. Fran raised his eyebrows but sat down anyway, drawing the afghan back up to make a nest.

"Shit, I'm sorry."

"Mm."

"That's—fuck. Fuck, that's messed up."

"Case of the final straw, I think," Fran said, shrugging, but his face was blank and cold. "My grandma—his mum—had just been told she had cancer, my mum was making noises about a divorce, he was massively in debt from this gambling addiction...and my dad was one of *them*, you know. One of those men's men. I was a nancy that he was ashamed of long before I came out. And my brother just let slip once, we were pissing about wrestling for the remote and he just went, 'Get off me, gay-boy, I'm not Joshua.'"

"Joshua?"

"Guy in my class I had a huge crush on."

"You didn't deny it? In front of your dad?"

"Didn't have a chance. I just went bright red. I was only about thirteen, you know how you are at that age. Someone even hints the guy you like is within a thousand yards and you go up in flames."

"Oh, fuck your brother."

"No, no, it was an accident," Fran insisted. "He'd known more or less since I had, years by that point, and he'd never breathed a word. Me and Ryan—I think that's actually what blew Dad's mind the most. Ryan was a proper man, that's how Dad saw him. Rugby and army cadets and never two minutes without a girlfriend. But we got on. We were like that." He held up crossed fingers and Jim grimaced.

"He sounds like a tool."

"He was. Total prick. Made sure to tell him twice a day. But he was my brother and he was in my corner. He used to come to my recitals even though he was deaf and couldn't hear a thing over the audience, even a nice, quiet, well-behaved one."

Jim grunted, grudgingly acquiescing.

"So yeah. I came out, got outed, whatever. And Dad just said, 'Figures.' And he walked out. Didn't come back. Police found him the next day, hanging down by the river."

"Fuck."

Fran hummed.

Jim wanted to ask. Wanted to know. Wanted to stir up whether Fran had blamed himself or hated his father for the overreaction. Wanted to probe into it, like poking a bruise. But something in that cold face told him not to. Told him to skirt around it and disappear.

So he did.

"I don't think Anthony knows how to tie a knot, so at least Oscar doesn't have to worry about that."

Fran barked a laugh.

"What about you?"

Jim grimaced. "Er. Yeah. Well."

"Yeah, well?"

"It's a bit complicated. When I have a girlfriend, I'm one of the family and everything's fine and normal. And when I have a boyfriend, I have a highly contagious disease and it's all a bit disgusting, isn't it?"

Fran chuckled, stretching out his legs. "That sounds familiar."

Jim raised his eyebrows. "Oh, your girlfriend wasn't a phase, either?"

"Nope. I prefer sex with men but relationships with women. You're a bit of an anomaly on the TV-and-food part."

Jim preened.

"Yeah, yeah. Egomaniac…"

"You're not."

"What, an exception?"

"Yeah. I have a thing for blonds. Don't care what kit comes with it, they just have to be blond."

"Natural or dyed?"

"Don't care. Blond."

Fran laughed.

"I'm serious! I've had one brunet in my life and even he had to start dying it."

"Did the carpet match the curtains?"

"It did after he was done in the bathroom."

"Ouch, no chance." Fran winced, cupping his crotch in an exaggerated fashion. "No way. The most you're getting out of me is a trim."

"I can live with that. I like the fluffy look."

"*Fluffy?*"

They started playfighting on the sofa, until Jim let his greater weight tire Fran out and they ended up cuddling on the carpet again, the cat prowling around their heads with inquisitive meows, probably wondering why they'd fallen off if they didn't intend on feeding it.

"So, what's Oscar going to do?" Fran asked quietly once calm had descended once more.

"No idea," Jim admitted.

"I want to tell him — her — them, I want to tell them that they can talk to me if they need to," Fran said, "but it could be awful if they figure out you told me."

Jim whistled through his teeth. "Well. There's, uh. There's one way."

"Oh?"

"Could swap a secret for a secret. Maybe if they realise we're having this thing — "

"This thing?"

"Whatever it is."

"According to you, it's a relationship."

"Eh?"

Fran laughed. "That day you stalked me to a cafe? You said a relationship was just someone you liked screwing, seeing movies with and eating with. Well — " He waved at the TV and the remnants of their dinner.

"Huh. I guess so."

It ought to have felt like a momentous declaration. The earth should have moved or something. But then Jim didn't have a romantic bone in his body, so he simply frowned blankly at the telly.

"Does that make you my boyfriend?"

"I don't know, are you fourteen?"

Jim snorted.

"If you need a name for it, your conqueror works."

"Please. My chattel."

"Oh, is it fancy words you want? Fine. You're my concubine."

Jim complained. Fran kept coming up with more and more outlandish terms. And it felt —

Nice. Just nice. Cuddling on the carpet. Being made fun of. A naked leg against his own, suggesting there might be some different playfighting in a bit.

It felt like it was something Jim had been looking for, even though he hadn't. Felt as if he'd found something he'd been missing, even though he hadn't known there was a hole.

Still, he pinched and called Fran a tart.

Couldn't let him go getting ideas, right?

Chapter Eleven

Oscar didn't say a word.

He looked a little brighter and the last piano lesson before the trip to Abu Dhabi or where-the-hell-ever filled the house with a jaunty version of *Clocks* that was sweet but also maddening as hell, especially when followed up with Patricia's key-banging. But in the end, the Sunday morning arrived without a whisper of a new name or the secret getting out, and the nearest evidence of their chat Jim was left with was getting an actual hug at the door before Oscar dashed off to the car.

"Your boys' chat go well?" Sarah asked.

"Yep."

"Will you tell me who it is he likes?" she whispered in a conspiratorial fashion and Jim gaped at her.

"*Sarah!*"

"What? Mum's right to know!"

"I can't breach guy code like that," Jim said severely. "What is said in guy talk *stays* in guy talk."

She rolled her eyes but let him alone. As she walked off down to the steps to the waiting car — of *course* they were taking the Merc, the bastards — Jim turned go back inside and found himself face-to-face with his brother-in-law.

"A quick word, James?"

Jim fought to keep his face impassive. Anthony's quick words were never good.

"I do appreciate your offer to housesit," Anthony said lowly, "but, ah, if you could…"

He trailed off.

"What? Remember to feed the cat you don't own?"

"What?" Anthony said blankly. "No, no, I mean…"

He coughed awkwardly and made a gesture that was completely unintelligible. Jim stared blankly.

"Please refrain from — using the house."

"Using the house?" Jim echoed flatly. "I live here."

"I mean in the…carnal sense."

Jim blinked.

Then it clicked.

"You don't want me to have sex in it?"

"I would prefer it if you didn't bring men home, no."

"You realise I'm bisexual, mate?"

"I — am aware."

"And what that means?"

"I know the definition of the word, yes," Anthony said irritably.

"But there you go with that whole men line again. What if I want to bring a woman over? What if I want to spend three weeks licking—"

"James!"

"Could you do me a huge favour?" Jim snapped. "One of two things, I'll take either right now as I don't reckon you'll manage both. Either stop assuming I'm gay, because I'm not, or stop equating literally everything I could possibly do with a man as filth. I'm also not married so any kind of sex is off the table in your book, right?"

Anthony pursed his lips like an angry housewife and Jim saw red.

"What is your fucking problem?" he demanded. "You wear a collar more often than I do, but it doesn't turn everyone in your flock into a judgemental prick!"

"Don't shout," Anthony hissed, glancing down at the car. Two out of three kids were staring.

"I'll shout if I want!" Jim retorted. "I'll have sex if I want! Don't know if you noticed in your backward corner of the world, but it's not exactly illegal! I could call about fifteen people right now and have them over for a good orgy the minute you're out that door and there is nothing you or anybody else can do about it."

"I forbid you from—!"

"From what? Go on, forbid me."

The spluttering noise died.

"Yeah, thought so," Jim snapped. "Don't act like your kids were left in the cabbage patch, either. Living proof you've done the nasty, so stop acting like me doing it is any different."

"My *wife* and I—"

"Yeah, my *boyfriend* and I," Jim mimicked. "I don't care what your book tells you. It's not *my* book. It's not *my* faith. So stop trying to use *your* rules on *my* life. You have a religion that says you can't actually enjoy sex, that's not my problem. I don't. *My* beliefs don't think men together are disgusting."

"Now look here, it's nothing to do with men toge—"

"Except it is!" Jim bellowed. "It always is with you! Pick one! Either you're a bigot or this is nothing to do with my sexuality and you're just too much of a coward to say you don't like me. Newsflash, dickhead, I don't like you, either! I don't like you looking down your nose at me all the time and pitying me like I'm something you scraped off your shoe! You might have conned my sister into thinking you're a decent guy, but me? I know what you are. You're a fucking hypocrite and one day, trust me, karma is going to run your dogma over flat, straight into the tarmac. And I hope I'm there when it happens, because the look on your face is going to be fucking perfect."

Jim stalked back into the house and up the stairs. For a moment, he heard Anthony come farther into the hall, then a muted shout that might have been one of the kids or might have been Sarah. There was a long pause, in which Jim waited on the threshold of his room, barely breathing.

And the heavy tread retreated.

The front door closed.

And Jim punched the wall.

The dent in the plaster made pain explode up his arm, but the rage cleared in a second. He sighed, flexing his fingers out. *Dickhead.* And a *gone* dickhead. Jim could waste time stewing or he could get busy striking back.

And Jim was nothing if not a pro at being an obnoxious twat when it came to Anthony Lovelace.

He tiptoed into the master bedroom, with its enormous bay window that overlooked the front of the house, and crouched behind the lace curtains, hidden, as the Mercedes turned on the vast gravel driveway. The gates shuddered and began to open, and Jim grinned. The minute that Sarah's car disappeared from view, Jim dropped the curtain and reached for his phone.

Me: Come over.

It was half past one in the afternoon. And, as usual on a Sunday, Fran seemed to be as faithless as Jim and answered almost at once.

Fran: What?

Me: Come over!

Fran: To Sarah's?

Me: Yep.

Fran: No lessons.

Me: They just left on holiday. No family. No servants – sorry, household help. Just you and me and a lot of rooms to christen.

Fran: You have a one-track mind.

Me: And you have a fantastic body.

Fran: Flatterer.

There was a long pause.
Then Jim punched the air.

Fran: Be there in 30.

He darted into the bathroom for the world's fastest shower and change of clothes. Loose and easy to remove. He ruffled up his hair into spikes, spending a good ten minutes perfecting them, and by the time he heard the buzzer go for the front gate, he was itching out of his own skin for a shag. Not even a good shag. That could come later, pun intended. Right at that minute, what he wanted was to get his rocks off and preferably as fast as possible.

Nothing like an empty house and a forbidden act to get the blood going.

Yeah, he wanted a fuck. Especially with Fran. But he also wanted to stick two fingers up to Anthony. If it was automatically inappropriate to bring men home, then Jim was going to be as flagrantly inappropriate as possible. There was *definitely* a screw on Anthony and Sarah's bed on the cards. If he could fuck a man in this house at least once every day for three weeks, then Jim was going to do it.

He released the catch for the gate and opened the front door to watch and wait. The car peeled right up to the front of the house and Fran got out wearing a pair of mirrored sunglasses and a black T-shirt that made his pale skin and obnoxiously blond hair glow like the surface of the sun. He looked hot, figuratively and literally, and Jim expected his hand to burn clean off when he reached out to touch him.

They tangled in a messy kiss in the doorway and Jim had to kick it shut behind them, clumsy and blind.

Who the fuck cared.

"Jeans," he said, pulling at the zip of Fran's aforementioned trousers. "Why are you wearing jeans?"

"Wasn't going to drive naked."

"Why the fuck not?" Jim asked and dropped to his knees.

He swallowed Fran to the root in one go. Didn't matter that he was still soft, tasted of cotton and smelled like the inside of a far too hot car. Jim wanted his dick and he wanted it now. He sucked clumsily until it swelled on his tongue and only when he was working at a hard shaft did he pull back and yank the jeans down pale legs to get some skin under his palms as well as in his mouth.

"Fucking *hell* —"

It wasn't the best blow job Jim had ever given. He just got a cheek in one hand, balls in another and sucked as if his life depended on it. Fuck the piano. He was going for a record on the oboe and Fran's gasping was better than any damned concerto in whatever-the-hell- major key. When Jim squeezed Fran's arse, it would trigger a groan like he was coming. When he rubbed the rough of his tongue over the head, he'd hear Fran stop breathing altogether. And when he rubbed a single finger behind his balls as though trying to find the seams, the shudder was more responsive than any instrument.

Sod Fran — maybe Jim was a musician after all.

It was quick and dirty up against the door and he pulled off to let Fran come on his face. The hot splatter was ridiculously hot, then Fran sank to his knees and licked it off Jim's face like a cat after the cream. And so they ended up in a sticky, sweaty mess on the hall floor, fused at the mouth in dangerous kisses and Fran's hands steadily working their way into Jim's board shorts.

"Wait," Jim said and the hands stilled.

"You're kidding."

"Move."

"Why the fuck would I move?"

The coarse curse made him laugh drunkenly.

"Done this room. C'mon. Kitchen."

"Kitchen?"

"Yeah. Wanna fuck your brains out on the kitchen floor."

"Fuck that."

His lower lip was seized between sharp teeth and bitten. Hard. The jump of pain made his dick obscenely hard.

"Living room. It's closer. Give me rug burn I'm gonna feel for days."

"Fuck."

They stumbled into the living room in a tangle of limbs. They didn't so much as lie down on the rug as fall, and Jim found himself wrestling for control. Fran was slippery, wriggly, all kisses and teeth and slick skin. Jim sank his teeth into Fran's neck hard enough to make him freeze and whimper and the soft cock in Jim's hand thickened noticeably.

"Fucking insatiable," Jim snarled and the cock hardened further. "What, you like me telling you that you're gagging for it?"

It swelled again and Fran groaned. "Fuck yes."

"Like a bit of dirty talk?"

Hands pulled at his hair.

"Oi," Jim said, shaking them off. He pinned them to the rug, both of those narrow wrists in one hand. He licked at Fran's open mouth and laughed at the glazed look in his eyes. "Want me to tell you that you're a whore? Because it's true. You've had yours, now it's my turn."

"Oh God, yes." Fran groaned, then kicked. The savage burst of motion freed one foot of the jeans entirely and he spread his legs. Despite sucking him off as though they were university freshers in their first gay club toilets, Jim hadn't noticed he wasn't wearing underwear.

"Right. Over you go."

Jim flipped him onto his front and spread his arse with both hands. He spat and heard Fran's low groan.

"If you rub yourself off on that rug," he threatened, "then I'll get a cock ring on you and you won't get another go all over this house."

"Fuck-fuck-fuck—*oh, Jesus!*"

The shout said that Jim had lost zero talent with his mouth. He didn't have lube, so he worked with fingers and tongue relentlessly, one hand under Fran's hips to keep that cock nice and hard for him and reduce the sly, sneaky pianist to begging. Literally pleading. Bargaining. Making any and every deal under the sun, if only he could come.

"Not yet," Jim said, then sat back on his heels and pinched one flushed arse cheek. "Stay right there. I'm going to get the lube."

"Oh, fuck, please—"

"Yes. Fuck. Pleasing fuck. Once I get the lube."

Walking was hard. Pun intended. He wanted to run, but couldn't. His cock led him into his borrowed bedroom like a divining rod pointing out sources of extra pleasure and he sadistically took both bottles as well as the condoms. Why not make a show of it? Lot of rooms downstairs, after all.

Fran had turned over when he got back. He was lying on his back, head stretched back to show that badly bitten neck, stroking himself in one lazy hand.

"Bad behaviour, that," Jim chided as he knelt between bent legs. "Maybe I should have brought that cock ring."

"You want me to behave, you're going to have to learn to make me," came the raspy reply.

"Yeah? Maybe this will help."

It didn't. It made him worse. Fran jacked himself almost frantically as Jim opened him up, and only stilled when Jim had rolled the condom on and caught both wrists again, planting them on the rug either side of Fran's face.

Their eyes were mere inches apart.

"*Behave*," Jim whispered.

That pale grey stare sharpened.

Focused.

Narrowed.

"Like hell."

Thighs smashed at his hips. Arms surged. An unstoppable force crashed into his chest and the living room tipped — then the rug was under his back. Legs straddled him. Fingers like steel traps clamped around his arms and slammed them to the floor.

And Fran said, "I told you, Love. You want to make me behave, you'll have to learn how."

Jim opened his mouth — and yelled.

It dissolved into a groan as a pressure like a vice sank down around his cock. Pleasure exploded in his veins. He gasped wordlessly at the ceiling as he was taken deep. Deeper than ever before. To the fucking root.

Then Fran stilled. Head thrown back. Chest heaving. Sweat standing out in glimmering drops in the evening light.

"Fuck," he breathed. "Holy fucking God."

"Move. Move. Please, God, move."

"I'll move when I want."

"You move," Jim gasped. "Or I'll turn us over and move for you."

A flash of laughter. Teeth. Fingers squeezed.

Then he moved.

The grip and slide was incredible. It was the tightest hand job of his life. It was heat so fierce it would burn them alive. It dragged Jim's entire soul to his dick and he'd fuck forever if it felt like this. He'd fuck till he starved if he'd starve like this.

But it was slow. The drag and drop. Too slow. He wanted to see power. Pistons. A *fuck*. He wasn't here to make love on the forbidden rug. He was here to fuck senseless.

With a jerk, he freed his hands. Fran ignored him, burying his own hands in his hair as he rode Jim as if he were nothing but a cock for hire—and Jim seized those narrow hips in both hands and *thrust*.

"Oh, fuck!"

"Yes," Jim panted as he began a punishing rhythm. The grace was lost. Fran collapsed over his chest. An ear came in range and Jim bit it until he tasted blood.

"Oh, fuck, yes, just like that, *yes* – "

Jim didn't know when he came. He didn't know when it ended. He didn't know when he lost the rhythm, or when they parted, or when the condom was slid off and the contents emptied onto his chest.

He only stirred again when he felt Fran sucking his nipple clean, the very edges of teeth teasing at his shattered nerves.

"Hello," Jim muttered, stroking that sweaty, fair hair.

Fran kissed the bruised nipple and smiled up at him.

"Hello," he rasped and cupped Jim's cock in one hand. "Want to take this to a bathroom and clean up?"

"Nope," Jim said and turned them in a strange, tangled hug, clasping his mouth to Fran's and tasting their mingled bodies there.

"Then what?" Fran whispered in the tiny gap remaining.

"Bed," Jim whispered. "Gonna climb all the way inside you and never come out."

"Okay."

Chapter Twelve

Jim could get used to this.

It was half-past-five on Thursday afternoon and Fran had just arrived as though he lived here. Rolled that red car through the gates, kicked the driver's door shut behind him and staggered up the steps with two shopping bags and a tower of binders.

"Please tell me you don't have to do work," Jim said.

"Not tonight," Fran said. "This is for the weekend."

Jim grinned, stole a kiss and took the bags into the kitchen.

That first Sunday had been frantic sex, and as much of it as Jim could manage. But there were several rooms left and they'd taken all the days since off to enjoy the incredible TV in the living room. Jim hadn't tried porn on it yet, but he could only imagine cinema screen–size cock was going to blow his mind. Pun intended.

But tonight, he had plans. He'd been shopping — not that Fran knew that — and designs on a very particular room in the house.

Namely, Anthony and Sarah's room.

Which had a four-poster bed.

"So I had an idea," Jim said as he unpacked the shopping and Fran dumped the binders on the kitchen table.

"Dangerous things. Best avoided."

"I want you to really think about it before you say no."

Fran paused in the act of ordering the binders. "Oh, hell."

"It's not that bad!"

"Then stop making it sound bad!"

Jim laughed, then abandoned the bags and caught Fran's arm. "Come on, let me show you."

He'd dumped his purchases on the bed in the master bedroom. Fran wrinkled his nose at the lacy décor but eyed the box curiously and, when Jim simply shrugged, plonked himself down and picked it up.

"A present?"

"If you like it, sure."

Fran smirked and opened it up. Jim had just put the stuff in a shoebox, nothing more, but he felt as anxious as if he'd left a ring in a proper fancy box. And it was anticlimactic when Fran lifted out the strip of cloth and simply looked blankly at it, plainly not understanding a thing.

"Okay?"

"It's a blindfold."

"Oh. *Oh.*"

"You said I might be allowed that one," Jim said awkwardly.

Fran chuckled, turning the strip over in his hands. It was smooth and soft and a rich, dark blue that had caught Jim's eye at once. Combined with Fran's hair and Jim's thing for blindfolds in general, it would get him going in about half a second.

"It's not the only thing."

Fran peered back into the box and drew out the other item between finger and thumb. He looked utterly nonplussed.

"It's the same thing?" he said questioningly and Jim shook his head.

"See the rubber bit?"

Fran turned it over, touching the padded lengths, but still looked blank.

"Sorry," he said. "My kink experience is pretty limited. This isn't all that obvious."

"It's a gag."

Fran simply blinked and Jim waited with bated breath. He wasn't one for ball gags. But a strip of cloth between teeth, under a matching blindfold? Hello, sign him up. Fran didn't seem so enthralled, though, and Jim chewed on his lip anxiously.

"I'd like to believe you just like the look of cloth on my face," Fran said slowly, "but doesn't this usually come with something else?"

"Well, ideally, I'd like to tie you to the posts, but you said no, so no," Jim said. "Although…if you don't mind tying *me* to the posts later, that would be fucking *awesome*."

"Deal," Fran said with a smirk but held up the gag. "But what was the other thing, before I even consider this?"

"This is the bit you need to hear me out with," Jim said.

"Okay."

"Going by the way you react when I bite you, you…kind of have a tiny bit of a pain thing going."

Fran said nothing.

"I wanted to...kind of...try that out a bit."

"Define 'a bit'."

"Nothing crazy," Jim said quickly. "Just—maybe scratch you. And if you liked that, then...I know this really awesome trick with a knif—"

"A *knife*!"

"Hear me out!"

"You are not fucking cutting me," Fran said sharply.

"No-no-no, that's the trick," Jim said hastily. "You get a blunt knife, like proper butter-knife blunt, and you freeze it. And the cold makes it feel sharp and dangerous and sexy, but in reality all that I'd be doing is dragging the flat of it over your skin. No risk. Promise."

"Don't care," came the flat reply. "No knives."

Jim bit his lip. "Okay."

"But..."

He waited hopefully.

"Maybe the scratching thing. You're not exactly wrong."

Jim grinned. "Yeah?"

"Mm. Ex might have exploited that a few times."

Jim dropped onto the bed beside him, taking the gag and rubbing it between his fingers. "I won't restrain you. Not even with my hands, promise. So if you don't like it, you can push me or pull my hair and—"

"I like to pull your hair."

Jim laughed. "Okay, hit me, then. And I'll stop. And it's really easy to take off. It's stretchy so you can just pull it away from your mouth with your hands if you need to."

Fran nodded slowly, still watching his fingers play with the cloth.

"Honestly? Can we park that for tomorrow or the weekend?" he asked. "It's a bit—I don't know. Bit heavy tonight."

"Yeah. Fine. Sure. Whatever you—"

"How about—"

And Fran was sliding into his lap, hot and warm and those full lips kissing his stubble like he wanted to map Jim's jaw.

"How about tonight, *you* wear the blindfold. And you give me a *proper* blow job. Not that clumsy thing at the front door on Sunday. That proper deep-throat action I got in the toilets at the cinema. I want one of those."

* * * *

Jim drew him in.

All the way in.

And right there, he stilled.

He couldn't see a thing. The blindfold had turned the world black and drowned Jim in the abyss. But he could feel. Hear. Smell. Taste. And these nerves were all amplified a thousandfold.

He could feel Fran's pulse on his tongue, rabbit-fast and frantic. There were fingers in his hair, slowly relaxing as Jim stilled. Petting. Stroking. A thumb dropped down to brush his cheek and send new nerves crackling into life like an electric charge chasing it for more. He could feel the ache in his jaw beating in tandem with the ache in his cock, and the thickness of the major vein trapped against his thigh an echo of the one he cupped with his tongue. The cold metal biting into his wrists dragged him from the hot safety of Fran's hips and yet the same heat dragged him right back. He hung between the two, still but for the careful, slow breathing.

And he could hear that breathing. Hear it in his nose and easing past the thick shaft almost blocking his throat. He could hear two pulses and, in the darkness, had no real idea which was his own and which was Fran's. The soft rasp of his hair against fingers as Fran stroked both hands to the back of Jim's head was like grass crunching in the frost, and the soft creak of the office chair like a door groaning in some old, abandoned house.

But it wasn't that which encompassed Jim so completely and tore him from his own body.

It was the smell.

Everything smelled like Fran. Everything. There was nothing but that familiar scent. The marker pens and wood smoke, the cotton and the aftershave, the gentle hint of wine from dinner and the heavier stain of tea that permeated him as though it had dyed his soul. It filled Jim's nose and mouth like it would never go away, and he drifted in it aimlessly. He was off-balance. He was held in place by the fingers in his hair. They could relax and let him go or persist and choke him. He was blind, and his forearms locked together behind his back, one over the other in the most useless position that could be managed. His cock was a pounding distraction in his jeans, pinned to his thigh and hurting with the need for release.

And yet he was utterly surrounded by Fran's smell. So he drifted.

None of it mattered. He could hear him, smell him, feel him. And somehow, simply because Jim couldn't *see* him, it turned Fran from a point in the world to the entire world itself. Fran was the universe. And Jim was utterly contained within that universe, whatever it wanted and wherever it went. There was no escape and there was no desire to. If there was an edge, a place where Jim could step beyond an invisible line and break free, then he wanted to know for the pure avoidance of it.

He wanted to be here, right here, for the rest of time.

So he relaxed when the pulse sped up too far and reached a warning point, a hammering where all the sound bled together into a hum. He relaxed when the little hitch sounded in Fran's throat and that high, gorgeous groan leaked out into the room. He relaxed as the sudden rush of release choked him and cut off his air and he relaxed through the spike of instinctive panic and the slow, sweet release of relief as his throat dragged it all down, and swallowed it without a murmur.

And he relaxed when Fran let go.

Sagged forward into his lap, letting the soft shaft slip from his lips, and nestled into a bare thigh as though it were home. He didn't hear the words. Didn't care about them. Nothing that could have been said mattered all — nothing *did* matter, except this.

Except the feeling of hands smoothing his hair.

Except the sound of a heartbeat slowing to happiness under his ear.

Except the smell of sensual satisfaction filling his nose.

Nothing else mattered.

Chapter Thirteen

There were sour faces in the car.

Jim felt free and easy. On top of the world andgetting higher. So maybe he didn't help, lounging in the doorway in jogging bottoms and a ratty T-shirt with a shit-eating grin on his face, but who the fuck cared? He'd spent three weeks having great food, in better company, and doing dirty, nasty sins in every room of the precious reverend's house.

And judging by the exasperated sigh Sarah aimed at him, said reverend hadn't been having the best of times in Barbados or wherever it had been.

"How'd it go?" Jim called.

Sarah grunted as she opened the boot.

"How did it go?" he repeated more slowly, as Anthony edged past him and vanished into the house.

"That's right!" Sarah shouted, like Jim wasn't even there. "Don't bother to *help*, oh no! Your precious parishioners might need you! Never mind your family!"

Ouch. Jim winced and decided to step in.

"Hey, can Uncle have a hug?" he asked, heading down the steps and opening the car door by Aggie's seat. She seemed utterly oblivious to any tension and crowed merrily. He freed her from the straps and hefted her up, groaning in an exaggerated fashion under the weight to make her laugh.

"And how's my favourite?" he asked, then shushed in her ear and blew on the shell to make her squeal. "Ssh, mustn't tell! They'll all get jealous."

She called him silly — maybe — and asked for biscuits, or beatniks, or picnics. He shifted her on onto his hip, took a bag with his free arm and waddled awkwardly into the house. As he set bag and baby down in the hall, Sarah stalked past and shouted at Anthony at full volume.

"Er, how was the holiday?" he asked Oscar.

Oscar shrugged and traipsed off upstairs. Patricia flounced through into the kitchen, presumably to watch her parents' suffering with her usual glee.

Jim looked down at Aggie, who stared right back up at him balefully.

"Huh. Okay. Guess it's just you and me, then, sunshine?"

He took the excuse to steal the TV to watch *Pingu* with her — in Jim's lofty opinion, far superior to any of this *Peppa Pig* bollocks — and made ever louder 'noot noot' noises with their black-and-white hero until the back door slammed and a shadow stormed past the window en route to the drive.

"There goes Daddy," Jim mused.

"Da," Aggie echoed blankly, then pointed at the screen. "Noot noot!"

"Oh, come on, that was a noot noot, not a *noot* noot…"

It took some time for Sarah to stop banging around in the kitchen and Jim suspected that the subdued quiet that fell later was due to a bottle of wine or two. But eventually he managed to ease Aggie off into a nap and tuck her into the armchair, then kicked his feet up and put on a quiet football match instead.

Only for Sarah to come in, makeup running, and switch it right back off again.

Great.

"So," Jim said, tossing the remote aside. "Not go well?"

"I want a divorce," she snapped, sinking down into the other armchair.

"Oh hell, Sarah, come on—"

"The whole trip, it was phone-phone-phone. He never once put it down. The WI need this, Reverend Cole is asking this, Mrs bloody Miggins down the bloody tea shop needs that!"

Her voice cracked and Jim winced.

"He just fobbed off the kids with handfuls of baht every time they whined and sat under a parasol using the resort Wi-Fi! I don't mind sharing my husband with God, but I do mind sharing him with the whole fucking parish!"

Jim winced, glancing at Aggie. Thankfully she had her thumb in her mouth and was still—miraculously—sound asleep.

"I swear to his fucking God, if he doesn't come back in here later with a bunch of flowers and a fucking apology and actually spend *time* with me, me and his kids—*his* kids, not just mine, *his*—then I'm walking out that fucking door!"

"Okay, seriously, you need to keep it down a bi—"

"Don't fucking tell me to keep it down!" she bellowed and threw the wineglass.

It missed spectacularly. It bounced off the sofa by Jim's knee and sent a spray of red across the white rug. Sarah burst into noisy tears and Jim groaned.

"Right," he said. "Right. Okay. I'll, er. I'll stick that in the wash, shall I?"

Could rugs *be* put in the wash? Jim didn't have a clue. But he lifted the coffee table anyway and gathered up the rug in his arms to dump it in the utility room. It was bloody heavy, a great big bastard, and he ought to have rolled it first, but too late. By the time he dropped it, his back was aching. And Jim was far too young to have a dodgy back, for Christ's sake.

The living room was quiet.

Eerily quiet.

How Aggie hadn't woken up was a miracle unto itself, but Sarah's sudden silence unnerved him and he beat a hasty retreat to make sure she wasn't doing something daft. And the minute he walked in, he realised the mistake he'd made.

Because in the empty space left by the rug was miles of pink carpet, and a single white spot.

Right at the edge, where the rug had just about covered it up. Right where Jim had wrestled Fran for top and sort of won but sort of lost at the same time. Right where they'd dissolved. Right where one of them – and Jim still couldn't tell who – had got cum on the carpet.

He'd meant to scrub it out.

Obviously, he'd forgotten.

And Sarah was sitting in absolute silence. Staring. Right. At it.

"Er," Jim said.

"You did, didn't you?"

"I did…what?"

She snorted. "Someone. A man. Or he did you. Here. In my living room. On my carpet. *When we told you not to.*"

She had mascara smeared all down her face. Her wineglass was still sitting in the middle of the floor. Her toddler was starting to grumble and growl in her sleep and there'd be a tantrum if any more noise was made.

Jim wanted to be the bigger man. He wanted to walk away.

But that little hiss dug into his skin and broke through.

When we told you not to.

"Yeah," he said. "I did. I invited a man over and we had sex. In here. And in the hall. And on the stairs. And in every room in the house."

Sarah lifted her face to his and her eyes were spitting fire.

"And I'd do it again," he spat.

She moved like lightning. Suddenly the wineglass was in her hand. Her hand was in the air. Her bracelet flashed.

And the glass exploded in a shower of shards by Jim's ear.

"Get out!"

Aggie began to scream. And Jim—got out.

He ducked into the hall and fled. Just ran. Bolted right out of the door. The overcast sky had broken and it had started to rain, but Jim didn't pay any attention. He paused at the closed gates for only a second before deciding to hell with it. The sharp spike of fear when she'd thrown the glass at him was already ebbing and as he scaled the wall and dropped down into the ditch on the other side, his temper started to replace it.

Get out.

Have a sex life in her house? Get out. Dare to like men in her house? Get out. Go against the faith of a husband she apparently wanted to divorce and who spent more time with his parish than his family? Get out.

Be *Jim?* Get out, get out, get out.

He couldn't do this. The revenge had been sweet, but suddenly Jim realised it wasn't worth it. It wasn't going to end. He'd do it again to spite her, so she'd scream again and come out with the same garbage, and it would just go on and on and on, forever and ever. He was turning back into the shit kid who'd nicked that car, who'd started that fight, who'd ended up in prison because he couldn't control the urge to be a fucking dickhead when people pissed him off.

He'd sworn to himself, that first night in prison, that he'd learn. That he'd do better. And he had.

But having sex in every room of the house just to fuck her off was the kind of thing he'd done back then and Jim didn't want to go back down that road. He couldn't. He'd done it once and it had been the biggest mistake of his life.

Slowly, the rain helped cool his temper. And everything else. It was bouncing it down, a layer of water hovering above the road from the force of it. He'd stormed out in his trainers and hadn't thought about grabbing his coat on the way out either and the reality was slowly pressing in on him as he drifted absently toward the village, lost in the thoughts turning over and over in his head.

He couldn't go back, not after that barney. Maybe not ever, if she was never going to realise what she was saying whenever she commented on his attraction to other men.

But he couldn't stay out here, either.

And the answer came to him naturally as breathing.

He had to walk half a mile to find a bus shelter and stood in its pathetic coverage trying to dry his phone enough to make it work. But once it did, the name was easy. Most frequent contact now — although he didn't usually ring it.

"Jim?"

"Hey, Fran."

"Everything okay?"

He grimaced. "Not really."

"You sound like you're in a bin."

"Bus shelter. Same thing."

"Okay. Er. Why?"

"Had a blazing row with Sarah. Um. Sorry, but can I crash at yours tonight?"

There was a rustling noise.

"Sure. You'll have to park on the next street, though. Imran over the road is getting married and everyone and his dog got invited, apparently."

"Um, I haven't borrowed the car."

There was a long pause.

"Jay."

The little nickname made Jim's stomach clench up, and in a very different way to the churning anger in the house.

"Where are you?"

"Fuck knows. Er. About half a mile into Totley. Or maybe Dore, I don't know. Bus shelter opposite some chippie. Andy's."

"Andy's Kitchen?"

"Yeah."

"Okay. I know it. I'll come and get you." Fran's voice was oddly gentle and Jim felt a little bit sick. Christ, he was a fuck-up, wasn't he?

"I can get a bus—"

"It's ten past eight on a Sunday and you're in Totley. What bus?"

Jim chuckled wetly. "Good point."

"It's going to take me half an hour. You good till then?"

"Sure."

He laughed when Fran made a loud kissing noise, then hung up. Leaning back to perch on the tiny bar that served for a seat in the shelter, Jim peered up at the brown sky rapidly turning black and wondered if he couldn't just go over to Fran's and stay there for good. He wasn't sure he could stay with Sarah anymore. Not if he wanted to stay sane. Not if he wanted to get another job and another flat and be a man, not the pissy kid who'd got banged up in a cell for acting like a twat whenever things got on top of him.

Maybe it was time to grow up.

And maybe part of growing was finally learning his lesson about his family. However much it might hurt.

Jim didn't have any money to go on a last-minute raid of the chippie and he doubted Sarah was going to come after him in the Merc in this weather, so he had little choice but to shiver, wait and fantasise about crashing at Fran's in the long term. He'd have to pay toward it, somehow. The dole didn't get him far, but it might cover his half of the bills. And he could sleep on the sofa, if Fran wasn't sold on sharing his bed. It wasn't as if they'd been going out long and Jim could see it might be a bit of a jump. But he didn't have anywhere else, or he'd already be there. And Fran was sweet like that. He'd let Jim stay for a *little* while, right, especially if Jim lent a financial hand around the house? Fran was a teacher; he couldn't earn much. It would help.

Whatever Fran's income, it was enough to handle speeding tickets. He turned up in twenty minutes, not thirty, and Jim sank gratefully into the warm car like it had come from heaven itself. Screw the Merc. He'd take a warm Ford Focus with a gorgeous driver any day.

"Thank you, Jeeves."

Fran laughed. "Charming. Where's my thank you?"

"You'll get it at your house."

"Fair enough. Want anything from the chippie?"

"Nah." Now he was in the car, Jim sort of just wanted a hug, wet as that sounded.

"Okay. Want a hot shower and a hotter shag?"

"Yeah, go on then."

"Deal."

They didn't talk. Fran didn't ask about the fight and Jim didn't volunteer any information. They simply sat in companionable quiet, the radio chirping between them and the whir of wipers a soothing rhythm against the thoughts chasing one another around Jim's head.

The street was packed out. One of the houses over the road was spilling music and light into the rain, a couple of pretty Pakistani girls in saris sheltering under an umbrella and having a smoke, doubtless out of sight of their elders. They waved to Fran and eyed Jim curiously, but he ducked his head and ignored them until the dark mouth of Fran's front door opened invitingly and he could shuffle in.

Much to the disgust of the little cat, which took one look at the water streaming off him onto the kitchen tiles and shot off upstairs with a hiss.

"Get yourself in the shower," Fran said. "I'll bring up a brew. Have you eaten?"

"Thanks, and yeah. To be honest, I'm just — tired."

In more ways than one.

"Then get showered and get into bed. Leave your clothes in the bath, I can stick them in the wash in the morning."

Jim went and did as he was told. The shower was heaven, the water drumming on his shoulders as if it was determined to beat the stress right out of him. He sighed and tipped his head up into the stream, revelling in the steam rising all around him. *Heat.* Christ, heat felt so good. Getting out took some effort, then he simply sat in the towel for a while, trying to massage the knots out of his own neck.

Knuckles rapped on the door.

"Yeah?"

"You okay?"

"Yeah. Sorry. I'll be right out."

"Just unlock this?"

Jim turned the lock over and Fran slipped inside. He was carrying a heat pack and Jim sighed as it was planted on the back of his neck.

"You looked haggard," Fran said and kissed the top of his wet hair. "Come on. Come to bed. I'll ask questions in the morning."

"M'kay."

It was heaven. Quiet, soft heaven. He didn't really remember much about the bed itself last time — too preoccupied with its owner — but he sank into warm softness, a mess of throws and blankets rather than a tidy duvet and pillow combination, and it all smelled of citrus fabric softener. There was a posh feather pillow and he tucked his face into it before sending an arm out in search of a more organic warmth.

"C'mere."

A soft laugh. He hauled.

Then they were cocooned together, hot spoons in a drawer full of cotton, and everything else—the rain drumming on the roof, the cat sitting awkwardly on his ankle, the echo of the wineglass shattering by his ear—

None of it mattered anymore.

He didn't have to be on his best behaviour here.

Chapter Fourteen

They left the curtains open.

It meant Jim was poked in the eyes by the sun at some unholy hour of the morning and turning over to escape by burying his face into Fran's shoulder blades didn't help. Mostly because then he was there and he sort of sighed in a sleepy way and his arse was right over Jim's lap...

The sex was slow and sleepy and utterly spectacular, then Fran squirmed free, complaining about a wet spot, and the next thing Jim knew, the sun was significantly higher in the sky and Fran was sitting on the windowsill, smoking.

"Don't you have work?" he asked stupidly and Fran laughed at him.

"It's Bank Holiday Monday."

"Huh."

He lay back and stared. If Jim had thought Fran looked heavenly at the piano in the sun, it was nothing compared to the view of him sitting on the windowsill, naked but for Jim's borrowed T-shirt, smoking a cigarette by the open pane. The sun bathed him in red and gold, his skin bright white but his hair transformed into liquid silver. For a split second as he tipped his head back and exhaled, the cloud of grey curling into the morning air, Jim couldn't breathe.

"You're a work of art," he croaked.

Fran laughed.

"Seriously. You could be a model."

A snort. "I did a bit, actually."

"Yeah?"

"Yeah, the odd cash-in-hand stint as a student. Used to have my picture up in a little opticians' place near Crystal Peaks. Can still find me on stock photo sites now and then."

"Why didn't you keep it up?"

"Oh, you need to be dedicated for that kind of thing."

He said it airily, like he was just slipping through life without a care in the world. Jim envied him.

"You could have been anything. A musician. An artist. A model. Why a French teacher?"

Fran smirked at the ceiling. "It pays. Art and music and modelling don't, not unless you're one of the very lucky few. And forgive me, but I don't find starving artist all that wonderful or romantic. I did my time in coffee shops and call centres. Even feral children are preferable to high street customers at Christmas."

"Good point," Jim said.

Fran flicked the stub out of the window and climbed down. He stripped the T-shirt back off and crawled over Jim's naked body like a cat on the prowl. Hot skin sank over him until Jim thought he might be scalded, but he tracked his hands up miles of magnificence anyway and caught lips in his teeth as a warning.

"Behave," he whispered.

"Make me."

"Maybe later."

They drifted together in idle kisses, Jim slowly exploring with his fingers for a potential second round once he'd mustered up the energy, but a thought was unfurling gently in the back of his mind to disturb the peace and eventually it slipped free.

"I bet you could have made a career out of anything."

"Not many careers in sex and smoking."

"Porn star's a career. Sex worker's a career."

"Mm, yes, but then you'd have to see me have sex with other people and I don't think you'd like that," Fran whispered, beginning to chew on his ear.

Jim's cock jolted.

"Oh, *hello*."

"Er."

Fran sat back, grinning. "So you *would* like to see me have sex with other people?"

"I have no idea," Jim said honestly. He blinked up at the god sitting on his hips, a little startled by the reaction.

"Imagine it," Fran murmured, sinking down over his chest and whispering in his ear. His nails kneaded Jim's chest in prickles of pain and pleasure. "Birthday present for a good friend, letting him have someone like me. Only you want to watch. Make sure everything's above board. And I'm liking it just a little too much, so maybe you need to remind me — "

Jim bucked. Twisted. Slammed Fran into the bed below him and clamped a hand around that clever mouth, squeezing when teeth gnawed on his forefinger.

"Shut up," he grunted, rubbing his fully recovered cock into Fran's hip. "Just—fuck. Fucking hell—"

Ankles locked over his back. He ought to get more lube. Get another condom. Get—

Inside.

In. Now. *In.*

Heat. Pressure. The squeeze was incredible. The groan under his hand and chest like thunder. Jim let go. Grasped wrists in his hands. Held them there on the bed, arm's-length, watching. Pinned Fran down and watched while he *fucked.* No other word for it but fuck. Short, hard, powerful, painful thrusts. He didn't have sex. He didn't make love. He fucked into him like the world was ending. The headboard was banging. There was blood on Fran's lip where he'd bitten it. Every yes was in time. It was like—like—

Like a storm breaking on the edge of the mountains.

Like the tsunami crashing into the city skyline.

Like an end.

Jim came in a white-out. His own breathing was scraping in his ears. He'd been electrocuted. Nerves jangling like shattered glass in a shaken bag. It ached to pull out. He was hot and wet and his skin was slick where it met Fran's. He felt numb. Distant. There was a hand around Fran's cock, but it might not have been his own. There was cum on skin, but was it his on Fran's, or Fran's on his? Fuck knew. Fuck cared.

He breathed.

Came round with a pulse under his mouth. Kissed it and felt it quicken. Smelled sex and sweat and skin.

He sank his teeth into the long neck that awaited him, and ground down until the grunt turned into the perfectly pitched whine.

"Fuuuuck, that's good," Fran sighed.

"Mm?"

"I like you best when you're rough."

"I'll m'ke a note," Jim mumbled. He tightened his arms. The body inside them coiled up and cuddled. He made a happy sigh and a face nuzzled at his cheek.

"I won't."

"Wh't?"

"Sleep with other people. Not my thing. Not up for that."

"S'fine," Jim mumbled. "That was — plenty."

A soft chuckle. A kiss brushed his cheekbone, then teeth began to mark it.

"Go look at Grindr later," Jim suggested, twisting his face away and tucking it safely into sweat-soaked hair. "Then I'll do you on the kitchen table."

"Deal."

He laughed breathlessly. "You're like — like Prozac for the soul."

"Am I?"

"Yeah. I felt shit last night. Now I feel like I'm God."

"Oh, bloody hell, don't go getting ideas…"

Jim chuckled.

"So, what happened last night?"

He grimaced. "Holiday wasn't so great."

"Oh?"

"Apparently Anthony obsessed about the parish the whole time and didn't spend a minute with Sarah or the sprogs, so she was in a foul mood when she got back. Then she figured out we'd had sex —"

"*What?*"

"Not *we*, like — me and someone," Jim said hastily.

The sudden tension eased again, although the languid looseness was well and truly gone. Jim butted his nose against the drying hair in a mute apology.

142

"I'm guessing she wasn't happy?"

"Understatement of the century. Started having a go at me, all of this 'we told you not to bring men home' and blah-blah-blah, and I lost my temper. Told her she was being a hypocritical bigot, told her I was—yeah, well, I said a lot of stuff. Then she threw a glass at my head, so I bailed."

"I take it she missed?"

"Yeah."

"Good." Knuckles found his ribs and Jim wriggled. "So what now? You going back later, or—"

Jim groaned. He rolled onto his back to stare at the ceiling. The plastering needed redoing.

"I don't know," he admitted. "I'm going mad in there. I feel like I'm turning back into that shit kid who—"

He barely stopped himself in time.

"Who what?"

"Crap."

Fran propped himself up on one elbow.

"Who what?" he insisted gently.

"Get ready to dump me," Jim said dramatically, then let out a huge rush of air. "That shit kid who nicked that car and got in that fight and went to prison."

There was a long, long silence.

A couple were walking past in the street arguing about someone called Graham. A dog was barking a few gardens away. The gutter was smacking the wall in the wind and probably needed repairing sooner rather than later.

But in the red bedroom, there was silence.

"D'you want me to go?" Jim eventually asked the cracked ceiling.

"I'd rather you explained that," came the gentle rebuke.

He groaned. "I was a dumb kid."

"Mm, going to need a *bit* more…"

"I was a stupid teenager," he said. "There's no excuse really. I was an immature shit. I mean, I can tell you *why* – no dad, and my sister being the golden girl, and me being thick as pigshit when it came to school stuff – but it's just excuses. I was just a shit teenager and I turned into a shit adult. And I was hitting up bars all the time, trying to get laid, trying to impress, because if I was attractive, then I felt good about myself. So one day I'm walking into town to get wasted and there's this car. A Lamborghini. Looked like it had come straight out of a spy thriller. And some idiot's left it with the engine running outside a house. Nobody around. I mean, looking back, where it was, it was probably some drug dealer's car and I'm lucky I haven't had my house set on fire or whatever, but anyway. I saw it and I thought if I showed up in *that*, I'd be able to get anyone I wanted. I'd be the most wanted man in Sheffield. So I took it."

He could still remember the car. Jim hadn't even really been one for cars – never had, apart from having sex in the posh ones – but even he'd loved it. It had been like driving a spaceship in the movies. The road might as well not have existed, she'd been so smooth. He'd have happily driven to a night out in Inverness in that car.

"So, I went to town in it, and sure enough, everyone's interested because I'm in that car. I didn't even go *in* a club for hours and hours, just kept going round and round in it and hitting on girls. And I hit on the wrong girl, didn't I? She's all flirty, she gets in my nicked car, then there's this thug at my side saying I've nicked his bird and a fight breaks out. Police show up, we all get slammed and of course they figured out I'd nicked the car, didn't they?"

"And you got prison for that?"

"Owner of the car didn't want it back and damages paid, he wanted me punished proper. And I'd been fighting. I mean, okay, that guy started it, but I went way overboard back. I told you, I was a shit teenager. I had a problem with my temper. I broke his arm in two places and I went after his mate, too, so I got charged and taken to court. And they gave me three months in prison. And—and you know how people say that's when they woke up and smelled the coffee?"

"Yeah."

"My first night in the cells, I woke up, but I smelled the wrong drink. I was scared shitless. I thought I was surrounded by rapists and murderers—well, okay, yeah, there were a lot of rapists in there—but I was scared. I was twenty-two, I was still living with my mum and suddenly I was in prison surrounded by psychos. And I knew once you were in the system, you might not get out."

"Obviously you did," Fran said softly.

"Took a lot, though. I tried to fit in at first. Got into fights. Mouthed off at the staff. I thought I had to, I thought the other prisoners would get me if I looked weak. And I got done twice more for brawling with the officers, so my three months turned into fourteen months—and *that* was the coffee. When I got turned out for court again and I heard one of the lawyers say, 'Another one.' That was me. Another one. I realised then if I didn't sort my act out, I'd stay in and out of prison forever and I didn't want to do that. I wasn't *bad*.

I had this temper problem. I thought I needed a penis extension car. I was just *stupid*."

He hesitated, swallowing against the memory of that dank prison cell and the echoing hallways. It wasn't the prison that had been the worst bit, but the exercise yard. It had looked tantalisingly free. It had looked like he could have just left anytime he wanted, and yet he had known the cold, hard truth every time he had gone out. He'd hated it. He'd have rather been locked in the cell twenty-four-seven.

"I straightened out, I got out, I got work, I had a few relationships, I stopped seeing my mum and hearing her bollocks about me being a gay-boy or whatever and I got better. I was doing great. And now—lately with Sarah, with the way Anthony looks at me, I feel like I did back then," Jim admitted. "Shagging in every room in the house to spite them, that's what I would have done back then. I punched the wall when they left and buggered up the paintwork, I haven't punched anything since I came out of prison. So, I've no idea what I'm supposed to do now. I can't stay there, but I've got nowhere else to go."

Fran sighed. He sat up, drawing his legs under himself until he was cross-legged by Jim's hip, drumming his fingers lightly on the sheets.

"At the same time, aren't you just running away from the problem?"

"What?"

"I agree that removing yourself from the situation can help, but it doesn't mean you actually learn to deal with anything," Fran said. "If your default is to snap and snipe back at them, then maybe you need to really sit down with them—or at least your sister—and explain more rationally why the way she's acting upsets you. Then you've said your bit, you've dealt with it instead of sidestepped it and you can beat a retreat without leaving it to fester and happen all over again."

"Might not," Jim mumbled. "If I'm not there—"

"And next time it's not Sarah who makes some remark about fancying men. Or the time after that. Or after that. You see what I'm saying?"

Jim grunted. He did—but he didn't really like it.

"Go home," Fran said, "and when Sarah's in less of a confrontational mood, talk to her. Really talk to her, don't snap or snarl, just lay it out really rationally how she and Anthony make you feel. Tell her what you just told me. And give it a little bit of time—say a week, a fortnight, whatever—and if things don't get any better, walk away."

"To where?" Jim said and Fran chuckled.

"You're already here."

Jim bit his lip. "Really?"

"Sure. I could do with some welcome home head every once in a while. If it falls through with Sarah, you can stay with me until you sort out a job and a new place."

Fucking hell. Jim really had landed someone from heaven, hadn't he?

He turned over, taking the entire sheet with him and burying Fran alive, burrowing his face into Fran's neck and chewing when he heard the laughter bubbling up.

"You can't be serious—"

"Ssh, this isn't sex, it's a thank you."

"This is not a—"

Jim bit. *Hard.*

"*Fuck.* Oh God. Um. You're welcome. Thank me some more. *More,* you ungrateful bastard…"

Chapter Fifteen

Jim was a coward.

He didn't want to face his sister. He didn't want to wander into some fresh-divorce minefield. He wasn't even up to seeing Patricia burning ants under magnifying glasses or whatever it was the little weirdo did when her tutors weren't watching. So, he stayed. All of Monday, even when Fran put those little glasses on and worked his way through a stack of exam papers, completely ignoring that anyone else existed on the entire planet.

Jim just — stayed.

But it came to an end Tuesday morning, mostly because Fran had no spare key.

"You can't stay locked in," he said. "Go out or go home. I'll text you when I leave work, if you want."

He dropped Jim off in town and drove on to whatever school it was he actually worked for, looking ridiculously fuckable in that three-piece suit. Jim wanted to follow him, not go home and be a reasonable adult with Sarah. But then he squared his shoulders. He had somewhere to go. Even if it was only temporary, he had another option. He could do just what Fran had said. Lay it all out in the open, exactly what he thought and what this arrangement was doing to him and walk away.

And if there was one thing Jim knew he was good at, it was walking away.

Walking *back*, however...

It was almost June and summer had arrived early. Sheffield was usually piss-wet and miserable right into August, but the sky was a deep cornflower blue and there wasn't a cloud to be seen. Jim found himself drifting off toward the city library and printing another stack of CVs, then taking advantage of the unseasonable dryness to patrol up and down all the main streets and drop off papers into every bar, restaurant and coffee shop he could find. He even tried a bookstore and a couple of independent traders on the off-chance, buoyed by the opportunity Fran had offered and the strong desire not to go home just yet.

But eventually he ran out of paper and out of excuses.

He found it at the bus station. Sheffield bus station was a weird little splay of bays and Jim always had trouble finding the right one. He'd wandered off into the wrong section and when he turned himself around to find the right bus, the poster caught his eye. A splash of bright and familiar colour in the bland blue and white décor.

Rainbows.

"Huh."

Pride.

Jim didn't go in for pride parades much. Didn't see the point. Afterparty was more his scene and he usually happened on it by accident. If he went out most summer Saturday nights, after all, then he was bound to hit up the pride afterparty sooner or later. Why bother with the march when all he wanted was the pretty people afterward?

But then, Jim had always known there were men like him.

Oscar didn't know that.

Glancing around to make sure he wouldn't be spotted — or, worse, taken for a bigot — Jim peeled the poster off the pole it had been stuck to and tucked it into his back pocket. Couldn't hurt to show it to the kid, right? And Jim would take him, if Oscar wanted to go. He'd suck it up for one day.

The bus out into Totley was rammed with pensioners, but the hot weather had reached the village, too, and Jim hadn't known the road out past Sarah's could be dry. The wall was hot as hell and he jumped down like a scalded cat, recovering briefly in the shady spot by the gates before loping up toward the house. His mind wasn't on Sarah at all anymore, but on the piece of paper in his pocket.

Thankfully, Sarah was busy. He could hear her on the phone in the study, talking financial bollocks with some client or other. Judging by the squeals of enthusiasm, Zoe and her youngest charge were in the conservatory and he passed Patricia and one of her long-suffering tutors in the dining room.

"Where's Oscar?" he asked and the woman blinked.

"I don't teach Oscar," was all she said and Jim rolled his eyes.

"Gee, thanks."

There wasn't any more noise, so Jim defaulted to the most likely spot—and sure enough, found the guilty party in his room, nose buried once more in a book.

"Don't want to go out and play?" Jim asked and Oscar jumped violently.

"Um. This is good, though."

"You can read outside, you know."

Oscar shrugged. Jim shrugged right back.

"Got a minute?"

Oscar blinked but nodded and put the book down. Some other tome way above his age, no doubt. He'd run out eventually. There couldn't be *that* many books in the world.

"I got an idea," Jim said, closing the door behind him and going to sit on the end of the bed. He held out the scrappy poster. "Saw this in town."

Oscar took one look at the rainbows and gasped.

"Figured you and me could have a day out," Jim said. "Tell your mum and dad we're going off hiking or something else they won't want to be a part of, and I'm going to give you some uncle-nephew advice about girls or something boring like that, eh? But instead"—he tapped the top of the leaflet and lowered his voice to a whisper—"we go have some uncle-niece time at the Pride parade."

Oscar bit his lip and stared at Jim over the top of the leaflet.

"There'll be lots of other families there," Jim said. "And there's going to be stalls. I checked it out on my phone on the way back. One of them's for a charity that looks out for kids like you."

The leaflet got scrunched up in Oscar's hands.

"There's other kids like me?" he whispered.

Jim's heart twisted. A sharp, agonising pain like a heart attack lanced right through his chest and his jaw sagged.

"Shitting hell, kid," he muttered. "Of course there's kids like you! There's bloody millions of them, all over the world!"

Oscar swallowed thickly. "I've never met one."

"You don't know that," Jim said. "There might be one right now at swimming or riding school who looks at you and thinks exactly the same thing. It's not tattooed on your forehead."

Shaking fingers started to shred the leaflet.

"We'll go on the Saturday for the big march," Jim said. "Just you and me. And we'll have a whole day out. There'll be loads of other families there and I've heard rumours on the grapevine—well, the Facebook page—that there's going to be a bouncy castle."

"I'm too old for that," Oscar said, but there was a hunger in his face that betrayed him.

"That's bollocks," Jim said. "The only reason *I* don't play on bouncy castles is they have weight restrictions these days."

Oscar laughed.

"Hey."

Jim leaned close to whisper in his ear.

"If you want to, we can even practice using a new name."

Oscar stilled.

"Just let me know what it is and I'll use it all day," Jim promised, then gently took the leaflet back. "Think it over, eh? And I'll stash this where your mum won't find it."

He moved to get up—only to stagger under the sudden weight as Oscar flung his arms around Jim's neck and hung on tight.

"You're the best," he mumbled into Jim's shirt and Jim's heart did that awful flinching again. Christ, he might need an ambulance at this rate. The urge to cry was getting pretty intense. Instead, he ruffled Oscar's hair, called him daft and prised him off.

God, what had he gotten himself into?

He headed into his room to dump his grubby clothes and hit up the bathroom for a shower before retreating downstairs on a feasting expedition. The one and only thing that Jim would grant his extended family was their taste in food. If Anthony was less devout about the one man, one woman thing and much more devout about the apparent need to feed anyone and everyone within a fifty-mile radius, Jim would probably have converted. Hell, he might even have *liked* him.

Okay, maybe not. But it would have helped.

A plan was brewing along with the tea and Jim glanced at the clock before fishing his phone out of his pocket. It was twenty-past-three. Fran might be done for the day—and if not, he soon would be.

Me: Hey, I have a question.

Silence. Jim shrugged and dropped his phone on the counter. Once he would have abhorred the carbs so soon before a pride afterparty, but to hell with it. Fran could help him burn it all off. And Fran seemed to kind of like the little paunch Jim was getting. He'd bitten it often enough when he got down there.

It took about ten minutes and three slices of honeyed toast before Fran sent him a question mark, and Jim smirked. A flicker of mischief lit up in his chest.

Me: Voolay voo cooshay avec moi say soar?

Fran: What?

Jim pulled a face and rang him.

"I *said*," he sighed, interrupting the bemused hello, "*voulez-vous couchez avec moi, ce soir?*"
"Good Lord," Fran said and hung up.
Then his phone beeped.

Fran: Copy and paste.

Fran: Voulez-vous couchez avec moi, ce soir?

Fran: Incidentally the question is in the formal, so this is more of a business proposition than a pickup line.

Me: Fine. Then I'll buy dinner. So. Voulez-vous couchez avec moi, ce soir?

Fran: Oui ;)

Me: I've got another question.

Fran: Go on then.

Me: Do you go to Pride?

Fran: Yes

Jim blinked. He—hadn't actually been expecting that. He knew the gay clubs in Sheffield fairly well and was certain he'd have noticed Fran. He was expecting a no, maybe something about being closeted, maybe just not having any gay friends to go with, maybe even a line about it being a bad idea for a teacher.

He hadn't really been expecting a yes.

Me: I don't usually but I'm taking Oscar to the parade.

Fran: That's a great idea!

Me: I have another one too, I think.

Fran: I'm listening…

Me: We could accidentally bump into you. And then you can find out Oscar's a girl, and he can find out you're rainbow friendly and he can talk to you about stuff too, and he never has to know I ratted.

Fran: !

Fran: What was all that about being dumb?

Fran: That's an awesome idea

Jim earned himself three kiss emojis, and smirked.

Fran: Reward for you next time you come over ;)

Jim: Next time? Ce soir!

Fran: Non.

Fran: Parents' evening at school.

Fran: I'm stuck here until eight.

Jim: Could meet you at yours at nine and shag you to sleep?

Fran: I will not need shagging to go to sleep, trust me...

Footsteps.

Specifically, heels. Sarah's heels.

"Oh. Jim."

Jim sighed, deleting the half-written, completely dirty reply he'd been composing, and locked the phone. Time to say it. Time to bare it all, without shouting, and —

"Do you have a minute? I owe you an apology."

Chapter Sixteen

Jim made coffee.

Sarah sat in silence at the table.

They didn't talk.

He sent one text to Fran — *can I tell Sarah about us?* — and ignored everything but the swirl of the teaspoons until there was no conceivable way known to faith or science that the coffee needed stirring any longer.

Only then did he pick up the mugs and take them to the table.

"Thank you," Sarah said quietly, then groaned. "I'm sorry about the other day. I just — snapped. Anthony and that damned holiday and then…then that."

Jim said nothing.

"I'm sorry for losing my temper."

His phone lit up. The preview showed the entire message.

Fran: Okay. Good luck x

"You can see where I'm coming from, though, can't you, Jim?"

"I hope not."

"What?"

"I hope I can't see where you're coming from," Jim said quietly, examining the wood. He scratched at it with a ragged edge of his thumbnail. "Can you do me a favour? Can we just do this thing for a minute where I talk and you listen and you don't say anything? Just for a little bit?"

He took the silence as a yes.

"I'm going to move out."

"Where are—"

"*Please.*"

She stopped.

"I can't do this," Jim said. "I appreciate you trying to help. I really do. And I'm grateful you let me stay. But I tried really hard—*really* hard—to sort myself out after prison and staying here is undoing all of it. I'm turning back into that spiteful, shitty kid again and I don't want to be him anymore. I was starting to like who I was before I moved in with you and now I don't anymore. So, I'm going to move out."

He sensed rather than saw her open her mouth, and shook his head.

"Putting it bluntly, you and Anthony make me feel like shit."

And the minute he said it, Jim knew that Fran was right. He'd let it fester. There was a sudden shock of something having released. Snapped. And not his temper, for once, but his resentment. He'd never realised that letting go could feel like—like letting *go*, stupid as it sounded.

"Ever since you let me stay, you've been on at me to be on my best behaviour. And when you do that, you're telling me that my normal behaviour is something you can't tolerate. And if I was playing drums at four in the morning, or watching porn in front of the kids, or teaching Aggie to curse, maybe I could understand that. But the only time it comes up is when there's even a hint of me being bisexual."

"That's not—!"

"*Sarah.*"

She fell quiet and Jim resumed smoothing out the nail against the table.

"I don't think you realise exactly what you're doing every time you say it, but when you say that I'm out of order for having my boyfriend come over—even when nobody's home—then you're *actually* saying it's out of order for me to have a boyfriend at all. Especially when you don't ever raise it about women. What you're saying is it would be fine if I had a girlfriend, but I have a boyfriend, so it's something to be kept out of the house."

"It wasn't a boyfriend, it was—"

"It *was* my boyfriend," Jim said firmly. "He was my boyfriend. He still is my boyfriend. And I went over to his place last night and we talked it over. And he said that I needed to stop just sidestepping it and tell you exactly how I feel and if I still couldn't stay here, I could stay with him for a while. So that's what I'm doing, because he's right. I explode and I shout and you shout and nothing ever changes because you think I'm being a moody shit and I never get you to actually hear what I'm saying. It just becomes one big row."

Silence. Finally, she kept quiet.

"So, I'm telling you now," Jim said. "Whether you realise it or not, all you and Anthony have done since I moved in is tell me that me being bisexual is bad. That part of who I *am* is bad. And it's turning me back into that spiteful shit who got himself into so much trouble because he was sick of being told he was wrong."

"Jim…"

"There's nothing wrong with me," he said. "And I'm sorry you can't see that."

He didn't want to look at her. He didn't want to look up and see the face. It would be the same face Mum had given him when she'd found out. The mixture of anger and pity and disappointment. And it was the pity that had gotten to Jim the most. The same look she'd give someone talking about their imaginary friend like it was real.

Poor soul, he really believes that.

That look.

He pushed back from the table.

"I've got a few job applications outstanding and stuff where I've put down this place as my address" — he resolutely skipped the true significance of Saturday — "so if it's all right, I'll stay just for a couple more weeks until those deadlines pass. Then I'll be out of your hair."

He didn't look over his shoulder. She didn't call him back.

But as Jim walked out of the kitchen, he felt as if something had been ripped away. Some oily film over his skin had been torn free and all the hairs on his arms felt clean and fluffy. Fresh out of the shower. Brand-new exfoliator. His entire body hummed with the release.

God, he should have done that years ago.

* * * *

" — then I said I'd be out of her hair and walked out," Jim finished.

"And that's it?"

"That's it."

"She didn't say anything?"

Jim shrugged.

They were sitting cross-legged in front of Fran's sofa, picking at mediocre Chinese food and ignoring a surprisingly good made-for-TV movie. Jim didn't think much of the takeaway, but the noodles were pretty decent.

"I can't believe she didn't say anything," Fran grumbled.

"That's kind of her thing," Jim said.

"Oh, a family of ostriches?"

"What?"

"Heads in the sand."

Jim chuckled. "I guess. I — oh hell."

His phone had started ringing on the arm of the sofa and as he twisted around to get it, the name made him wince.

"Speak of the devil and she shall appear. Hi, Sarah."

Fran hit the Mute button and stole Jim's carton.

"Hi, Jim. Are you — are you at your boyfriend's?"

"Yeah."

"Oh. What's…what's his name?"

Jim raised his eyebrows. "Why?"

She hiccupped. Jim grimaced. He hoped it was wine and not crying.

"I've been thinking about what you said," she mumbled. "It's not — I'm not like that. You know I'm not like that."

"I don't," he said flatly.

"I'm not!"

"Then why do you keep saying it?"

There was a long silence.

"I get it that it's against Anthony's beliefs," Jim said quietly, "but you know what, it's against my beliefs for a man to marry someone young enough to be his daughter. I kept my trap shut, didn't I? I came to the wedding, didn't I? I could still be happy for you."

She made a little noise.

"I'm not asking you to wave flags at Pride, Sarah, I'm just asking you to leave me alone," Jim said tiredly. "I'm an adult. I'm going out with another adult. It's not right you lecturing me about it as though the kids might catch something off me."

"I didn't — I didn't think you had anyone serious."

"Does that make a difference?"

"Yes."

"Does it?"

There was another long pause. Slowly, Fran's hand inched across Jim's knee toward his beer bottle. Jim slapped it away and gave him a look.

"*Behave!*" he mouthed.

"Make me," Fran whispered and stole it anyway.

"Git."

"What?"

"Not you," he said quickly.

"Is he — is he there? Your boyfriend?"

"Yes."

"You should, um. You should invite him over. For dinner or something."

Jim rolled his eyes. "What, suddenly you'd like to meet him?"

"Yes."

"Really?"

"Look—look, honestly, Jim, what you said today really hurt."

Jim bit back the urge to snap at her.

"I'm not like that. Maybe…maybe I've come off a bit like that, but I'm not. I know—I know Anthony's got his hang-ups about…you know, gays and whatnot, but I'm not like that. I'd like to get to know him. If he's important to you, then—then he'll be important to me, too, won't he?"

Jim raised an eyebrow, glancing at Fran out of the corner of his eye. "Er. I don't know that he'll be too interested in coming round for tea."

Fran smirked into his carton.

"Why not?"

"I just don't think it'll help," Jim said awkwardly. He had a feeling Anthony *really* wouldn't like knowing the piano teacher was batting for both teams. "I feel awkward enough with you right now, I don't want to drag Fra—erm, drag him into it, too."

She went very quiet.

Then she said, "Jim."

Oh, hell.

"When—when did you meet him? Your boyfriend?"

"A while ago."

"Before or after you moved in?"

Jim sighed. "After."

"Oh my God," she said. "Did you—? Are you—?"

Pause.

"Are you at Francesantonio's house?"

"Fran's, and yes."

Her voice almost vanished. "Oh."

Jim winced and waved at Fran. He cocked his head.

"I think you might lose a customer," Jim whispered, so quietly that Sarah would hopefully miss it.

Fran rolled his eyes. His glasses slipped a little, almost falling off the end of his nose, and he pushed them back up with a spare finger, still burrowing around in the stolen Chinese carton.

"I have others."

"So you and—you and Fran, then?"

"Yes."

"He's—like that, is he?"

Jim closed his eyes. For a moment, the temptation hung in front of him like the apple before Eve. *He's like that, is he?* Jim could hear the contempt. The disgust. He could hear it, even if Sarah herself couldn't.

Then he breathed out.

"He's bisexual, if that's what you mean."

There was another one of those long, yawning silences.

And Jim knew then and there that he'd done all he could. He'd made himself clear. He'd faced the issue head-on. And Sarah was not going to hear him.

He made his excuses and hung up.

Chapter Seventeen

Jim decided to stay until after the Pride parade.

He didn't want to let Oscar down and he wasn't totally convinced Sarah would let Oscar come out with him if he'd moved out already. So, he gritted his teeth and told himself it was just until the weekend.

Thankfully, Saturday rolled around *fast*.

Things had been silent and awkward, so Jim was a little surprised by the knock on his bedroom door at seven in the morning. He half-expected his sister. But it wasn't Sarah itching for another talk, it was Oscar asking if they couldn't go already. He had to be persuaded into breakfast and sat twitching and fidgeting all the way through.

"I've never seen him so excited about a hike," Sarah said suspiciously and Jim laughed.

"Don't tell," he whispered, "but I might have sold it to him that there's still land mines in the old army testing grounds in the valley. He thinks he's going to see a rabbit get exploded."

It was sufficiently dumb and boyish and Sarah smiled just as Jim knew she would. It was thin around the edges and she wouldn't look at him, but at least she smiled.

Unbidden, Fran's little story crept back into his mind and he wondered if Anthony and Sarah were really as bad as Fran's father. They were such pushy parents normally that a hike would be derided as a waste of time, time Oscar could have spent with extra piano lessons or studying his textbooks. And Jim was a little surprised that his revelation hadn't ruined the whole thing. But apparently Sarah was sufficiently worried about her so-called son to overlook it and any display of normal boyish behaviour was plainly wonderful in their eyes.

Jim could only hope she'd see normal girlish behaviour the same way.

He wasn't allowed to borrow the Merc or the BMW because of the supposed mud, but he *was* permitted to take out the rarely used Freelander on the condition he got it washed before they came back and bagged up their dirty shoes. The bag of hiking gear was dutifully tossed in the back, then Jim slammed the boot and forgot the bag existed.

"We'll bring you back some stray animals!" he shouted out of the window, but the moment they peeled out of the electric gates, Oscar turned on him with the widest smile — hell, the *only* smile — that Jim had ever seen on his narrow face.

"I want to get my face painted!"

"Gotcha," Jim said, giving him a thumbs-up. "I snuck some T-shirts into that bag. You want to get your hair done, too? Pretty sure they have a stall for hair stuff."

"Just my face," Oscar said. He kicked the glovebox. "Uncle Jim?"

"Yeah?"

"Why are you coming to the parade?"

"Because you want to go and I think it'll be good for you."

"Yeah, but like…why did you know about it?"

Jim snorted with laughter. "Are you trying to ask if I'm gay?"

Oscar went pink.

"Answer's no." He left it a beat, just to be a dick. "I'm bisexual."

"You like boys and girls?"

"And people who aren't boys *or* girls," Jim added peaceably. He geared himself up for an explanation, but to his surprise, Oscar didn't ask that.

Instead he said, "Do you like Mr Carr?"

Oh.

"Your piano teacher?"

"Yeah."

"Yeah, he's nice."

"You look at him like you like him."

Jim snorted with laughter. "You little sneak!"

"Well, you *do*," Oscar said heavily.

"Yeah, yeah, all right. I do like him."

Oscar fidgeted again. "Mum said he can't come and teach me anymore."

Jim groaned. Christ. Fran hadn't mentioned that.

"She says he's too busy for us."

"It's not that," Jim said. "Your parents found out something about Fran they didn't like and fired him." At least, Jim was certain that was the case. Fran wasn't the type to drop teaching a kid because his parents were shits, right?

"What did they find out?"

"They, uh, they found out he's like me."

"Bisexual?"

"Yeah."

Oscar blinked. "So — so he likes men, too?"

"Yep."

"Have you told him you like men? Have you told him you like *him*?"

"And back to you!" Jim said loudly. "Do you want to march in the parade or just watch from the sidelines?"

Oscar tried to get back on the subject of Jim's love life, but Jim stubbornly resisted and eventually managed to keep them on track. Parade was nixed in favour of watching, and Jim was persuaded into letting Oscar sit on his shoulders. Ten-year-olds were too heavy for that malarkey in his opinion, but the way Oscar's face lit up when they reached the west side of the city and began to see rainbows hanging out of shop windows killed any protest Jim might have had.

"Uncle Jim — "

"What?" Jim asked as he stuck the parking ticket on the windscreen.

"Can I wear this?"

Oscar had gone rummaging in the bag in the boot while Jim had paid for parking, and turned out a skirt. It was obviously one of Patricia's — Jim vaguely recognised it as one of her church skirts. It was purple velvet, pleated and utterly revolting, but the hope in Oscar's face was too fragile to break with the truth about how ugly it was.

"Sure," Jim said instead. "Though I don't think it'll match your shoes."

Oscar didn't care about yellow trainers clashing with a purple skirt. He barely let Jim bully him into the back seat of the car to change and bounced out again the minute the skirt was in place. And Jim grudgingly had to admit that Oscar hadn't quite hit the age where it would start to become obvious what he'd been assigned. Stick a couple of clips in his hair and he'd pass for a little girl well enough.

And he knew it, too, by the huge smile on his face and the way he slid his hand into Jim's even though he'd been refusing to hold hands for years.

"Can we go get our faces painted now?"

"Whoa, nobody said anything about *my* face."

Everything was still being set up. People were starting to gather for the parade and Jim forked out for a couple of Greggs pasties and found a good spot near the park entrance to watch all the floats go in. Oscar went quiet again, but not the miserable quiet that had been haunting the house for weeks. It was a fascinated quiet as he drank in the sights. Music and balloons, colour everywhere, a couple of drag queens scolding a young volunteer they obviously knew from somewhere or other, a lady on stilts nearly as tall as the shops that lined the commandeered road. Jim had expected questions, but instead he got a clingy hand and a wide-eyed, adoring stare.

"Excuse me, do you mind if I just pop my pram here?"

He turned at the request and smiled at the elderly lady who'd spoken.

"Sure," he said and waved at the toddler in said pram. "She'll get a good view from here."

"That's the idea," the lady chirped. "Her mum's marching. What about you?"

Jim tugged on Oscar's hand. "Here with my niece. It's her first one."

Oscar beamed. The lady beamed right back and held out a hand.

"Lovely to meet you, sweetie. I'm Maggie."

Oscar answered her without missing a beat. "I'm Juliet."

Jim committed it firmly to memory.

"Is your mum or dad in the parade?"

The smile dipped a little. "No. S'just me and Uncle Jim."

"Juliet's hoping to meet some kids her own age," Jim said. "And I'm here to admire the view."

"Ooh, my son's just the same," Maggie clucked. "It's a shame, too, he used to have a lovely young man —"

They talked queer families for a while until the crowds swelled properly and the throngs between the barriers started to form a line. Street vendors were wandering up and down and usually Jim made it a rule not to buy any of their overpriced tat, but Juliet was so enthralled by the fake rainbow flower necklaces — they probably had a name, but Jim didn't know it — and nearly burst into tears when she saw someone selling gender pronoun buttons that Jim didn't have the heart to say no. So he was nearly twenty quid poorer by the time the parade kicked off but shrugged it off at the glee on Juliet's face.

Fucking hell, he was going to *kill* Sarah if she fucked this up.

Jim wasn't much one for parades. He didn't like political parties of any colour being there, exploitative cunts. Banks and boutiques trying to sell their crap under rainbow lettering had always pissed him off, too. He preferred to stick to the afterparty, but he had to admit, the blasting music was nice. Maggie's granddaughter started jiggling in her pram and Jim found himself bopping on the spot, too, as the floats cruised back, all the cheesy-pop anthems battering them from every corner. And as Lady Gaga faded away toward the park, a marching band came after her, bracketed by the gayest bunch of coppers Jim had ever seen, mincing about in their uniforms and plainly loving it, and some stony-faced soldiers who'd obviously been told to keep their dicks in their uniforms until at least five o'clock.

And in the middle of the marching band—

Jim's jaw dropped at the flash of white.

"Uncle Jim, Uncle Jim, it's Mr Carr!"

No kidding. In skinny jeans. Dancing. With a bloody great trumpet sticking out of the front of his face, and Jim had been totally wrong. The statue at the piano had been a pathetic imitation of heaven. *This* was what an angel looked like. Dancing in the daylight, eyes closed, drinking in the music and the crowd and the *life* like that was what he lived on. His fingers flickered on the instrument, his feet twisted on the road, he turned and swirled and moved like oil through water. He made Jim want to dance, too. He made the whole world look grey and pathetic by comparison. He was *alive* in the rawest form, living and breathing and so obviously, patently, wonderfully, brilliantly happy in this cascade of colour and shouting and human life smashed into one tiny space for one tiny day.

Jim's heart stopped beating.

"Make him wave!" Juliet cried. "Uncle Jim! Make him wave, make him wave!"

Grey flashed. Sliding toward them as the band got closer. And Jim cupped his hands around his mouth and bellowed.

"Francesantonio!"

Eyes stopped. Focused. In a breath between notes, a wide smile flashed their way. Another musician looked and laughed, slipping behind him and throwing up an arm as though they were lending it to Fran and waving on his behalf. He smirked around the mouthpiece but never paused, never broke away from the music. Juliet laughed and waved back and Jim felt the dumbest smile wash over his face.

Then they were gone, marching away to the gates, still dancing, still swirling, not just a group of people with a bunch of brass, but the very embodiment of music itself. Music as it should be. Echoing, reflecting, amplifying, purifying, glorying life itself.

His heart started up again. It stretched inside his chest like it wanted to follow.

Then Juliet turned on him, hugging him tightly around the middle.

"Mr Carr came to Pride!" she shrieked and Jim laughed dumbly.

"He sure did. Hey, shall we see if we can find him later?"

"Yes!"

She was itching to move after that. They abandoned the last quarter of the parade, letting Maggie and her teeny-bopper granddaughter have their few inches of space at the barriers to wait for the marching mum, and dived into the crowd. Jim ended up having to pick Juliet up after all in the melee and could only set her down again once they were finally in the bag-search queue for the enclosed park where all the stalls had been set up.

Frankly, Jim was looking forward to the grass and a good, long drink.

"Uncle Jim?"

"Please don't tell me you need the loos," Jim said, grimacing at the wall of people ahead.

"No." She beckoned and he leaned down. "I don't like Juliet anymore."

"Okay," Jim said, quietly relieved. Patricia was bad enough, who needed a Juliet? "What do you want to try now?"

"Charlotte."

"Okay." That was much better. "Charlotte. Kick me if I forget."

"'Kay."

It took an age to get through bag search and they were waylaid by Charlotte spotting the face painting people and wanting to get a butterfly. Jim managed to scout up some glittery butterfly clips for her hair as well and took a photo of her on his phone once she was complete, beaming like a thrilled five-year-old rather than a terribly serious ten-year-old and finally looking like the kid she actually was.

Only then were they permitted to go and find Fran and show him the monster that Jim had created.

It wasn't hard. Marching bands were popular at Pride and a cluster of little boys wanted to bang the big drum. Fran was sheltering in the shade of a tree, laughing with a couple of other band members, the trumpet long gone and a pair of mirrored sunglasses shielding his eyes from the blinding June glare. Jim grinned and waved, then stumbled as Charlotte wrenched her hand away and went pelting over the grass towards him.

"Mr Carr, Mr Carr, *look!*"

Fran didn't get much chance to look. He got one of those back-breaking hugs of his own, the *oof* audible even at Jim's distance, and he blinked down in surprise, lifting his shades to the top of his head.

"Oh my God," he said.

"Fran, Charlotte. Charlotte, Fran."

"Charlotte," Fran echoed blankly, then smiled. "Okay. Charlotte it is. Did you bring Jim to Pride, or did he bring you?"

"I brought him," Charlotte said and Jim rolled his eyes.

"Sure," he said. "Whatever floats your boat, flower."

"We saw you playing!" she enthused. "I didn't know you could play trumpet. Can you teach me?"

"Er," Fran said. "Your dad doesn't want me to come over anymore."

Jim scowled. Fran shot him a look and quietly shook his head.

"But if I asked nicely, and he said yes, would you?"

"Sure," Fran said.

"C'mere."

He stooped and Charlotte whispered in his ear. Slowly, a smirk bloomed across those narrow features and white-grey eyes pinned Jim in place as he looked up.

"*Does* he now?"

Jim felt a creeping flush rising in his neck.

"Charlotte —"

"That's *very* interesting. Thank you, Charlotte."

She grinned up at Jim and it wasn't the pure happiness one. It was the devil incarnate. It was one she must have inherited from Sarah, because Jim knew full well he'd flashed that grin around himself a time or two.

Oh, hell.

"Come on, monster," he said. "Let's leave Mr Carr to his music. We're going to get some candyfloss or something, you want anything?"

"I'm good," Fran said, holding up a bottle of Sol. "Have fun!"

They'd barely gone ten metres before Jim's phone beeped in his pocket and he slid it out once he'd stuffed some candyfloss down Charlotte's neck and unleashed her on the bouncy castle for a bit.

Fran: Apparently you like me.

Jim raised his eyebrows. Bloody kids.

Me: Tell me something I don't know.

Fran: All right. Here's something you don't know. This is the one night of the year I go clubbing. So to quote the cheesy song I will never again admit to liking...

A pause. Jim waited with bated breath.

Fran: After the afterparty? ;)

Score.

Chapter Eighteen

Jim headed back out at ten.

It had been depressing as hell to watch Charlotte miserably wipe her face-paint off and slowly put all her new things into the bag, never to be seen again. She'd sniffled as she'd changed back into her trousers and nearly burst into tears when Jim had put the bag in the boot, their gatherings hidden in their unused hiking gear.

"Hey," he'd said, squatting down by the side of the car to peer at her face. "I know it sucks. Believe me, I *know*. But you're still Charlotte, okay?"

"'Kay."

She'd retreated back into her shell by the time they got home, sat quietly through dinner and wouldn't answer any of her mum's questions, and scuttled off to her room as soon as possible. Jim hid the bag in the back of his wardrobe and tried to put it out of his mind.

And by the time he went back out to meet the taxi at the gates at ten, he'd almost succeeded.

He'd been there. He'd snuck around and been bisexual in private. The way his mother acted — the way Sarah acted — he almost still was. But he was an adult now. If he wanted to go out and get smashed and shag blokes, then guess what? He was going to go out and get smashed and shag blokes. Especially blond pianist blokes who danced like they were a waterfall, all thunder and beauty.

And maybe Jim wouldn't shag a bloke like that. Maybe he'd make love to him.

"Oh God," Jim muttered to himself. "You are *so* fucking gone."

The cabbie was in high spirits and clearly knew exactly what the club Jim wanted was. He prattled on about some gay storyline in a soap Jim didn't watch, confided that he thought his kid was gay and asked if coming out parties were a thing.

"Not really," Jim said. "Just take her to Pride. She'll love it."

The club was heaving and he had to text Fran a meeting point before going in. He hadn't put much effort in. Tight jeans for a good bum, but a loose T-shirt because hey, he'd probably lose it anyway. Hadn't shaved, either, because he had a theory that Fran had a thing for his stubble and Jim wanted to test it.

So he waded to the bar, did six shots to get himself started, then dredged up a memory of those long fingers around a bottle of Sol and bought two.

Go out, check.

Get smashed, in progress.

Now for the bloke.

The club had a cage, because of course it did. And there was Fran, a beacon in the dark. Jim stared without a trace of self-consciousness and half the club was with

177

him. If Fran had come in with a shirt, it was long gone. The jeans were painted on and white as his skin. If Jim had never sucked him off, he'd still know the man's measurements. The dancing was wild and energetic, drunk and frenetic and completely fucking sexy. As Jim waded through the crowd, he started to pick up the detail. The glitter on Fran's skin. The missing glasses. The shimmering blue eyeshadow. The white paint on his lips. To his shock, Fran was wearing a pair of deep blue high heels as well and, with a jolt, Jim realised he just might have a thing for that.

Interesting.

He looked glorious. And there was a palm hovering near his bum as he wiggled. He was precariously hugging the edge of the platform, one leg hooked around a cage bar like a professional pole dancer and there were a couple of guys stroking his calves. Jim couldn't blame them. He wanted to get Fran out of those jeans with his teeth.

But he also couldn't let it continue. So he pushed himself between them, caught a knee and yanked.

White flashed. Fran looked down. Jim's breath caught.

The eyeshadow, the paint, the glitter—they turned those eyes into a pre-dawn sky. The lip of the sun just inching above the horizon. The deep blue dusk was pouring away up his face to his hair and the future lay right there in his wide, staring eyes.

Then he smiled and the sun came up.

"Come down!" Jim bellowed, holding up a beer.

Fran beamed, took it and stepped off the cage.

Just off. Right off. He fell and Jim barely caught him. And couldn't say a word before painted lips mashed his own and he laughed into a kiss that tasted heavily of vodka and gin.

"You're trashed," he shouted into an ear and had his own licked.

"Dance with me!"

It wasn't dancing, it was a tight hug and gyrate kind of deal. Jim kept one hand possessively on Fran's bum, though it didn't do a lot to ward off other hands, and they swapped booze through kisses until the bottles were empty and Fran was pulling himself back up onto the cage.

"Come on!"

Jim's head was starting to feel fuzzy and it smeared the crystal-clear edges of Fran's face. But it just made him look all the more beautiful and Jim followed him up above the crowd, slithering into the cage to trap him in the bars and dance, kiss, touch, steal whatever he could while Fran was lost in the music. He was totally transformed. The sardonic eyebrows were soft, the stuffy suit abandoned, the cultured clip of his consonants slurred and sweet. He looked his age and Jim could suddenly slot the two people together. The pianist and the porn star. The man who'd come undone in a toilet cubicle for him, but then pluck at piano keys and use fancy words to tell him that Jim had ideas above his station.

There wasn't a station.

There was just — Fran.

Fran, an incredible contradiction in terms. He could be a high-class prick and a low-class lover. He could be whatever he wanted and he was sliding his arms around Jim's neck and biting at his throat, rubbing his hips up against Jim's, smearing Jim in makeup and glitter and the sticky residue of booze on unwashed shot glasses.

Jim wanted him.

He found an ear. Shouted a suggestion. Was turned down.

"It's too early!"

Jim thought. Shouted another suggestion. Got a laugh, a hand in his and a change of direction.

Drunk on sex, Jim went down on his knees in the alley behind the club and worshipped. And drunk on love, he followed Fran right back in, right back to the cage, right back to the shots and the Sol, and never took his eyes, his hands, his focus, from the angel he'd found at the piano.

* * * *

There was a Jamaican steel band rehearsing in his head, and not only were they practising for a stadium, they were bad at it.

Jim might not have minded if the hangover had at least sounded nice.

But his own heartbeat was smashing his skull from the inside out and something — other than Fran's dick — had crawled into his mouth in the night and died. His spine hurt. His feet were blobs of dead matter on the end of concrete legs.

Jim. Felt. *Shit.*

"Kill me," he told the pillow.

"'Fter you," came the sleepy reply.

He wanted a hug. But he was too hot. And not in the usual smouldering sense. Physically, stickily hot.

"Fuck!"

He shot from the bed. The room tipped. He slammed off the wall and into the bathroom and threw up in the bath. Toilet was two inches too far.

"Fuuuuuck," he groaned.

His memory was patchy. He could remember eyeshadow. Giving head behind the club. Fran shouting at someone in the taxi rank for putting their hand in Jim's back pocket. Getting kicked out of the cab halfway back to Fran's for necking in the back seat like teenagers. A kebab—wait, had they eaten a kebab or just talked about it? Jim had a very fuzzy recollection of legs around his waist but wasn't sure if he'd had sex. He winced. If they had, he was willing to bet they'd skipped the rubber. *Balls.*

Slowly, he levered himself off the edge of the bath. Gargling tap water helped. Slurping a pint of it right out of the tap helped, too. Glancing down revealed he was a mess of bruises and glitter. A smeary lipstick mark encircled one nipple, but it was red, not white. The other one had been bitten so hard it was swollen and he could vaguely remember Fran licking it afterward.

Christ.

He'd not been that bladdered for a good year and a half and it felt bloody good and bloody awful.

He showered. It helped clear some of the fog, if not the pain, and by the time he shuffled back into the bedroom in a stolen towel, Jim felt sort of human. Fran had vanished, though, and he could hear a washing machine clunking downstairs, so he followed the noise to find all their clothes in the wash and Fran leaning sleepily up against the microwave, nursing a mug of coffee. He wasn't wearing his glasses and squinted at

Jim in a manner that suggested he'd lost the contacts, too.

"Hey," Jim said, offering a kiss. It was sleepy and sticky and sweet. "Do you feel as shit as I do?"

"Yep. Worth it."

"Did we fuck? I can't remember."

"My arse says yes."

"Oh. Er—"

"And no, we forgot."

"Oops." Jim rubbed the back of his head ruefully. "Er. If it helps, I don't think I have anything."

"S'fine." Fran yawned widely. "Our own stupid fault if you do. C'mere."

Another muzzy kiss was exchanged. Fran felt hot and sleep-flushed, almost sticky. There was blue smeared all over the top of his face, and a savage bite mark on his neck. Looked like Fran hadn't been the only one paying attention to nipples.

"I want bacon."

"I got eggs."

"That'll do."

"Do you remember that guy?"

"What guy?"

"The guy who felt you up in the smoking area?"

"No?"

"I think I punched him."

Jim snorted with laughter.

"Yeah, well, not gonna lie, I wanted to write my name on your bum when you were doing your thing in the cage."

"What thing?"

"Practically poledancing."

Fran stared blankly and Jim laughed.

"Trust me," he said. "I've seen the strip acts do a shoddier job."

"Thanks, I think."

"What was up with the shoes?"

Fran shrugged. "They looked good."

"No kidding. Can I persuade you into them again?"

"Not in public."

"Don't want them in public."

That earned him a laugh and another kiss, followed by a soft chew on his jaw.

"Maybe," Fran allowed. "They hurt like hell."

"Oh, you won't be walking around in them," Jim promised. He caught narrow hips in both hands and backed Fran into the counter, nosing at his neck. "Can we go back to bed? I want to remember it."

"No chance," Fran murmured, tilting his head for better access anyway. "I think we might have forgotten anything but spit. I'm sore as hell."

"I can kiss it better?"

"Hmm, that might work…"

They were interrupted by the sharp peal of a phone. Jim's phone. And something clicked in his head.

"Anthony called you."

Fran blinked. "What?"

"You've not been to the house since they got back from holiday. And Oscar said you weren't teaching him anymore."

"Oh."

"So Anthony called you."

Fran grimaced. It broke in half with a wide yawn. "Yeah. On my way to work, day after you told Sarah about us."

"What did he say?"

"Not much."

"Fran —"

Grey eyes flashed. "No, really. He didn't say much. He said, 'Your services are no longer required.' Then he hung up on me. That was it. Boom. Fired."

"That son of a —"

Fran snorted and looped his arms back around Jim's neck. "Let him. I have other private lessons. It was just a bit of extra cash on the side. Your contribution to the mortgage will cover it, if you stay here."

The anger went a bit fuzzy around the edges. Like Jim's heart, all melting and soft, when Fran reached up to kiss —

The phone started ringing again.

"Fuck's *sake.*"

Fran laughed. "Just answer it, you idiot."

Jim groaned, glancing over his shoulder to the jackets abandoned at the foot of the stairs.

"Go on. Probably your sister wondering where you are."

He grumbled but kicked the coats with his toe until his pocket appeared, then bent over to pick it. Fran slid a hand between his legs, the cheeky fucker, and Jim squeezed his thighs before straightening up.

And frowning.

"What the fuck?"

Anthony calling.

"Anthony's ringing me," he said stupidly.

He couldn't remember Anthony ever ringing him. *Ever.* They only talked when strictly necessary. Jim preferred to pretend his God-bothering brother-in-law didn't exist and Anthony liked to do the same for his bent one.

"Hang up or answer it, that's driving me mad," Fran grumbled as he poured another coffee from the jug.

Jim rolled his eyes but answered, figuring that if Anthony was calling, it was probably something serious.

"Anthony?"

"Uncle Jim?"

His blood ran cold. The tiny voice was familiar. And feeble. Sniffling.

She was crying.

"Charlotte?"

"Where are you?" she whispered. "Can you come and get me? Can I come and live somewhere else with you?"

"Hey-hey-hey, what's up, flower?" he asked, dropping his voice. Out of the corner of his eye, he saw Fran stiffen. "What's the matter?"

"I told Mum."

He closed his eyes. *Oh fuck.*

"What did you tell Mum, flower?"

"I told her t-that we went to Pride a-and I have a new name a-and—"

She started to sob and Jim's stomach clenched like an iron fist had reached down his neck and seized all his organs in an icy grip.

"Ssh, it's all right," he said. "It's okay, flower. Hey, I'll come right back, okay? We'll sort this out. You and me, right? Remember our pinkie promise?"

Fran vanished up the stairs. A moment later, a pair of jogging bottoms and a T-shirt hit the railings and Jim seized them. He wedged the phone between his shoulder and ear to keep talking as he fought his way into the borrowed clothes—too small, but they'd have to do—and shoved his feet into his shoes, sock-free.

"Charlotte? Calm down for me, flower. I'm coming home," he said as Fran rummaged car keys out of a drawer and walked right out of the front door, barefoot and shirtless and wearing nothing but his pyjama bottoms. "I'm only half an hour away. Where are you?"

"In my room."

"Okay, you stay in your room, okay? It's going to be fine, I promise."

"Mum *cried*."

"Mums are silly like that," he said. "My mum cried once because I broke a glass. It's just a mum thing, don't you worry about it…"

He'd wanted to hang up, but it only felt safe to do so when they reached Totley and she'd stopped crying. Then he swore, throwing the phone onto the dashboard.

"I'm going to fucking kill Sarah!" he seethed.

"What's happened?"

"Charlotte told them. This morning, I think."

"About being Charlotte?"

"Yeah. And she said that Sarah cried."

Fran hummed. "Well. It *is* a shock. Maybe — maybe Charlotte thought they'd react just like you and she's upset they're not thrilled."

"I swear to God if they've said anything —"

He dragged a hand down his face. The hangover had dulled to an angry throb in the back of his head. He'd kill them. She'd been so damn happy yesterday, like a normal kid for once in her life, and now this. He was going to absolutely murder them.

"I don't think I should come in," Fran said as he pulled up just shy of the gates. "It might just complicate things."

"Hate to say it, but you're right," Jim muttered. "Thanks."

He leaned over for a quick kiss and Fran tugged his hair.

"Let me know how it goes. And if you need anything. Or — Charlotte, is it? Or if Charlotte does."

"Yeah. Thanks."

It was cold out and he had to jump the wall. He heard the car pull away as he headed up the drive and he had to steel himself before unlocking the door and letting himself in. It was like his own coming out all over again. He half expected to find his mum on the stairs, scowling at him and calling him difficult.

He didn't expect the silence.

It was eerily quiet. Slowly, he toed off his shoes and hung up his coat, hovering at the bottom of the stairs. Sarah would probably be in the kitchen. She was always in the kitchen on Sundays. But Charlotte was in her room —

He went for the room.

The door was closed, something usually forbidden by the overbearing mother of the household. Jim knocked softly and cracked it open when there was no answer.

"Charlotte?"

A lump under the duvet stirred. Jim sighed and shut the door behind him, creeping around the carpet to kneel by the frame.

"Hey, flower," he whispered, laying an arm over the top. The lump wriggled under it but didn't make a noise. "C'mere. Come on, come here."

He shifted up. A face, still hidden, buried itself in his shoulder. The borrowed T-shirt got damp and Jim didn't say a word. He just hugged and waited it out, hoping that Fran was right. Hoping it was just an overexcited ten-year-old gushing about her big day and not getting the thrilled response she wanted.

But somehow he knew it wasn't.

He just knew. The look on Anthony's face when he'd asked for help for Gabriel. The hesitance over bringing men home. The way Mum would talk to him only if he had a girlfriend. The way Sarah just wouldn't talk about it, about any of it, about any of their history since they'd stopped being close little kids and started being distant, cold adults.

He *knew*.

"Hey," he whispered when the crying finally stopped. "Do you know where I've been?"

"No," came the tiny whisper.

"I've been to Mr Carr's house."

"Really?"

"Yep. You were right. I like him. And he likes me. And I stayed the night. 'Cause of you."

Sod it, he'd update Fran on the lie later. Whatever did the trick.

"You know, Grandma's going to be so mad at me."

"Grandma?"

"Yeah, she doesn't like it when I have boyfriends."

A wobbly sniffle. "Why?"

"Because she's a daft bat. She thinks — get this — *she* thinks you can only like girls *or* boys. How dumb is that?"

A giggle escaped and he nudged the top of her duvet-covered head with his nose.

"She's all happy when I have girlfriends because the phase is over, but then, oops, I fall over a gorgeous man and she gets mad again. And Mr Carr is *lovely*, so Grandma's going to be really mad."

"She's going to be really mad at me, too."

"Probably. You know what Mad Grandma looks like?"

"What?"

"One of them bullfrog things. All puffed up. She swells up like a balloon, *poof!* I reckon if you prick her with a needle, she'll explode. Shall we try it, next time she swells up?"

"Yeah."

The head emerged. Jim ruffled her hair and she buried it back in his shoulder, but—thank God—didn't start sobbing again.

"I told them we went to Pride and Dad got upset and said you shouldn't have taken me and he'd talk to you and I said I wanted to go and he said I was too young to understand and I said—I said—"

Jim could imagine very well what she'd said.

"It doesn't matter what you said," he settled on. "You're too young for the clubbing and the afterparty, but the parade is for everybody. And you're not too young to know what you are. Don't let anybody tell you there's an age for this, because it's bollocks. Some people know from being teeny tiny babies and some people don't figure it out until they're Grandma's age."

"Nobody's Grandma's age but Grandma," Charlotte said with childish conviction and Jim snorted with laughter.

"Up until the year before you were born, *her* mum was still alive."

Charlotte fixed him with a look that plainly said he was a complete moron for believing that grandmothers had mothers and Jim rolled his eyes.

"All right, madam. Look. I'm going to go and talk to your mum and dad. Okay? You going to be all right up here for a bit?"

"Yeah." She picked her duvet. "Um. Can—can we go—later, can we go out?"

"Where do you want to go?"

"Dunno. Just out."

"Sure. Tell you what. Now it's all out in the open, why don't we go and see if we can find you some books like that lady at the Mermaids stall told you about?"

She brightened up a little bit at the prospect of books. "Okay."

"You get ready and I'll go and have a word."

He shut the door behind himself again, figuring it best to keep Patricia out of Charlotte's space for the moment—though, by the quiet, the little monster had been whisked off somewhere by the nanny. Probably along with Aggie. Aggie was still young enough to screw with Sarah's exact nature and the lack of toys and chewed things everywhere suggested the rampaging wildebeest of a learning-to-run toddler had also been removed.

Well, at least Jim didn't have to worry about shouting loud enough to scare the Jesus out of a baby.

Truth be told, he was faintly surprised to find Sarah home at all, sitting at the kitchen table with a vacant look in her eyes. Anthony would be at church and Jim figured he'd insisted the nanny and the other brats went, too, given the morning's revelations, but it was odd that Sarah hadn't joined them. It would be like her to flee from the conflict.

But no, there she was. Sitting at the table and staring right through him as he walked in. As if he weren't there. As though he didn't exist.

Slowly, he pulled out a chair and sat down.

"Charlotte called me."

Nothing.

"She told me what happened."

Nothing.

"Said you cried."

Nothing.

Jim bit his lip. "Sarah. C'mon."

She blinked. Twice. Then glanced down and took a sip from her visibly congealed coffee. Jim grimaced.

"Talk to me."

"You knew."

He sighed. "Yeah, I knew."

She didn't say anything else and a flicker of frustration sparked in the pit of his stomach.

"I knew she was acting weird and I asked. And she told me. And I said it was fine, because it is. Isn't it?"

And there was the question.

"Fine," Sarah echoed flatly.

Jim waited.

She repeated it again and he still waited.

And eventually she said, "I don't know."

"I do."

Her gaze shot up and hit him full in the face. Jim stared right back, every muscle in his chest clenched and ready for the fight.

"It is fine," he said. "She's been miserable for months and we all know it. You said yourself she was acting strange. But when I took her to Pride yesterday, when she saw all these other families with two moms and trans daughters and everything else, she was happy. She was *normal.*"

Sarah winced.

"That's not normal."

Jim clamped down on the sudden rush of anger. He closed his eyes and breathed. This wasn't about him. He could rage and smash cups and shut Mum out all he wanted. But he needed to help Charlotte. He needed to stay this time.

He needed to be on his best behaviour.

"Okay," he said. "Let's say it's not. Let's say she's weird. So what?"

Sarah blinked.

"So what if she's weird," Jim said. "She was happy. She wasn't hurting anyone. She went from being this miserable little soul to a perfectly happy kid. She got her face painted, she played on the bouncy castle, she *laughed*. I don't think I've seen Charlotte laugh since she was knee-high. You know what, if I were a dad – or a mum, whatever – I'd want my kid to do that, instead of looking like a wet weekend. So what if she's a bit weird?"

Sarah's fingers tightened around the cup and she didn't say a word.

"She's your kid, Sarah."

"She."

"Yeah. She. She's still yours. Doesn't that matter more than anything else?"

There was a long, drawn-out silence and Jim took a deep breath – and played the card that he never wanted to admit was even there.

"I'm still your brother."

Her head jerked up.

"You still let me stay," Jim said quietly. "You didn't close the door on me, even though you hate what I've done and what I've become. And you know, most of that is my choices. I didn't choose to be bisexual, I didn't choose to fall in love with Tom or Gabriel or – " He checked the final name of unacceptables. "But I chose to drop out of school. I chose to steal that car. I chose to get into that fight. I made shit choices, *choices,* and you still came when I called. You're still my sister. And Charlotte's still your daughter."

Her face shivered.

Crumpled.

Then she finally put her cup down, put her hands over her face and burst into tears.

"Oh, hell."

He'd never been able to deal with tears. Well, okay, he *could.* But it made him weak. Jim was a sucker when it came to people crying. He'd do anything—say anything—to make it stop. If he was brutally honest with himself, it was the real reason why he couldn't bear to see his mother anymore. Because she cried and he found himself wanting to fix it, instead of holding the ground he'd rightfully taken.

So his resolve was swept away and he got up to come around the table and hug her.

"I don't know what to *do!*" she wailed and Jim groaned, stroking her hair.

"You go upstairs and you say exactly that," he said. "You tell her you're scared for her and you don't know what to do or what comes next, but you also tell her— really loud and really clear and again and again and again—that she's still your kid and that you love her. Because you *do.* I know you do."

Whatever dam had been holding back the floodwaters broke. She howled. She howled as though she was in physical pain and clung to Jim's neck as if she would be swept away. He simply…held on. His heart hurt and his throat closed and his vision blurred, too, but he held it back and held on for dear life. And for the first time in twenty-six proudly atheist years, he sent up a prayer. Just in case Anthony was right. Just in case Jim had missed the mark.

Dear God, please let her understand.

"I'm scared," she croaked. "Anthony's so upset, he's furious, he was already talking therapy when he went out to work, and what do I tell Patricia — and the tutors, and what about schools, what if he has to go back to school, and I've seen the papers, he'll want to be chopped up, he'll want all that surgery like your ex did, they're going to chop up my little boy — "

"Hey-hey-hey, ssh." Jim rested his cheek on her head and sighed. "Come on, it's all right. It's okay, it's all right, it's *fine* — "

"It can't be fine, it can't be — "

"Yes, it is," he said. "You didn't see her yesterday. She was *happy*. Do you get what I'm telling you? I let her wear some butterfly clips in her hair and I was telling everyone she was my niece and her name was Charlotte and people just smiled at her and accepted it, and she was *happy*. That was all I needed to do. That was it."

"That's never it, it's never it — "

"It might be," Jim said quietly. "Nobody knows. *She* doesn't know. And she doesn't need you to have all the answers, she needs you to hold her hand while she figures them out for herself. It's just like homework. You can't just *tell* her the answer. She has to figure it out for herself and she needs you to tell her she's doing a great job."

Slowly, the tide washed out again. He fetched tissues. She blew her nose, louder than a sailor swearing in a stormy harbour, and Jim quietly fixed a brew. When it was delivered, she frowned at him.

"Fuck, Jim, when did you grow up?"

He shrugged. "I don't know. Maybe this best behaviour lark rubbed off."

She smiled wanly.

"God, I'm terrified. You've seen the papers. This is going to be hell."

"Yeah, it will." Jim shrugged. "That's why she needs to know her family is with her. Which means you need to go upstairs, right now, and tell her that. Tell her that her mum loves her. Because I've *been* there, Sarah, I've been right there and right now? Right now she only knows one person in the whole world loves her, and that's me. Everyone else? Not a clue."

There was a long, long pause.

Then Sarah pushed back from the table and went upstairs.

Chapter Nineteen

Jim stayed out of it.

He texted Fran a couple of times and hid in the living room with Zoe and the brats. Patricia peppered him with questions that he ducked and he busied himself with Agnes. She was still far too young to have any idea what was going on – she didn't even talk yet, beyond 'mama' and 'oh-oh', which was apparently Zoe, and he concentrated on trying to get a 'Jim' out of her, or even an 'uncle'. It was a reprieve. And all the while he kept an ear out for tears or shouting upstairs and got only a long, grim silence.

By the time Zoe went to make dinner, and he heard the electric gates creak at the end of the drive, nobody had gone storming out in tears and Agnes had managed an 'unky'. And Jim was pretty sure that was going to be the highlight of his day.

Anthony came in with a face like thunder. Usually on a Sunday, he fussed over the baby and wanted to tell anyone who'd listen about his sermon. But he stomped straight upstairs and slammed into the master bedroom without pause and the uneasy silence returned for the next hour, until Zoe came hesitantly into the living room and said dinner was ready.

"Do you want me to get them?" Jim asked.

She looked enormously grateful and he handed over Aggie before heading up the stairs like a man going to his own execution.

Jim knew exactly how men like Anthony thought. This would all be Jim's fault. He'd let this dirty queer live under his roof and now he'd infected one of the children. Maybe Anthony wouldn't think in terms quite that stark, but that was the line of reasoning. Without Jim around, Charlotte would still be Oscar. Jim had been talking about boyfriends and taking her to Pride parades and getting her muddled up and confused. It would all be Jim's fault.

So he wasn't entirely surprised to stick his head around the bedroom door with the message that dinner was ready only to be told, "I want you out of my house."

Anthony was sitting on the edge of the bed, holding his dog collar in his hand and staring blankly at it. But the look he gave Jim was full of venom and Jim stared blankly back.

Then shrugged.

"That's a conversation you need to have with your wife," he replied and ducked back out.

Charlotte's bedroom door was still closed.

Taking a deep breath, he rapped with his knuckles — then popped open the door when he got no answer.

He found mother and daughter curled up on the bed together, peering at Sarah's phone. Both had very obviously been crying, but Charlotte gave him a wobbly smile and budged up. He squeezed onto the tiny bed to join them, almost squashing his niece entirely, and squinted at the screen.

Then groaned.

"Sarah!"

"You look cute," Charlotte opined.

It was a baby picture. Him as a fat toddler wearing a frilly bonnet his nan had made for him. Sarah as a four-year-old wearing a horrific dress made from the same kitchen curtain-style material. They were both beaming, because children didn't know any better. Their nan was beaming, too. Jim had always regarded these photos as evidence that she'd been a complete sadist.

"I was just telling Os — Charlotte about Nan putting you in bonnets so she could take us both to the ladies' loo."

"She was a weird old bat."

"Jim!"

"What? I was a baby! Who cared what loo I was in?" he objected, but he squeezed Charlotte's arm and smiled at her. He'd not missed the little check and the right name, either. Whatever had been said, maybe Sarah wasn't going to be the mum he feared. Maybe she'd not take after their mum at all but be a new breed unto herself. "I actually came up to say dinner's ready."

"Oh my God, I totally forgot! And it's Zoe's pay day as well — "

Sarah was up and out of there in a flash and Jim shifted to sit up and give Charlotte a hug, ruffling her hair as he let go.

"How'd that go?"

"Okay," she mumbled.

"You and your mum going to be all right?"

"I think so. She — she cried again. And she said it was scary and…and that she didn't like it because it's going to be hard for me, b-but if…if it makes me better to be Charlotte than not, then…then she'll say it, too."

"She says she loves you?"

"Yeah."

"Do you believe her?"

Charlotte nodded, then slid her arms around his waist and squeezed tightly. Jim rubbed her back until she let go, hearing the thanks without her saying a word.

"Come on," he said. "Let's get some food down our necks. I'm still hungover and haven't had a meal yet."

"Why?"

"Because you called me all upset so I didn't stop to have lunch with Mr Carr."

"Is he your boyfriend now?"

"Yeah."

Charlotte slid her hand into his as they went down the stairs together and Jim was saved from answering if he was going to move in with Fran by reaching the kitchen and the stony silence of the people assembled around the table.

Well, most of them.

Aggie was cooing at her mashed potato as if it would answer back and Patricia was busy making sure her beef was *quite* dead, the squealing of the knife on ceramic ear-splittingly painful, but Anthony sat with his hands folded as if in prayer, staring off into the middle distance with the blankest look that Jim had ever seen on his face, and Sarah was blowing her nose and looking utterly morose.

"Er," Jim said. "Well. I should go —"

"Sit."

Anthony's voice was hoarse. Jim sat automatically, then rolled his eyes at himself for obeying. Slowly, he reached for the gravy boat. Well, if he was here…

"When will you be moving out, James?"

Jim's fingers stilled on the china. Sarah's head jerked up.

"What *are* you talking about, Anthony?" she snapped.

"This is too far," Anthony said blankly. "I was willing to extend the hand of charity to a man in need, but—"

"*Charity?* He's family!"

"He has taken advance of living here to—"

"We need him here," Sarah snapped. "*I* need him here. And it's my house, too, so don't you go saying—"

"My name is on the deed, and—"

"To hell with the deed!"

"Sarah, please."

"Don't you dare, don't you dare do this! I know you, I know what this is about, you think this is all Jim's fault."

"If he hadn't taken Oscar to—"

"It's nothing to do with that. You *know* Os—" A beat. "You *know* Charlotte's been miserable, long before Jim moved in. We both knew something was wrong—"

"This is not a solution! He is conf—"

"Maybe he—she—maybe! But so what! If this makes hi—her *happy*, then—"

"Don't be ridiculous, it's unhealthy and—"

Charlotte was gripping her fork with white fingers. Patricia was staring in abject fascination, gaze switching between her parents and her older sister and slowly putting the pieces together. Jim quietly offered them both gravy and watched the argument beginning to boil over.

And as he put the gravy boat down, he interrupted.

"Did you sack Fran for being bisexual?"

Sarah stopped mid-sentence, jaw sagging. Anthony's eyes bulged.

"That's nothing to do with you."

"Except it is," Jim said, "given I'm his boyfriend and it came right on the heels of you finding that out. I'm just curious. Did you sack him because he's sleeping with me, or did you sack him because you didn't want a bisexual man teaching your kids?"

There was a long pause.

"It's inappropriate," Anthony said eventually.

"What is?"

Another silence.

"I think you think this is catching," Jim said, "and I've always tried to leave your faith alone, but, quite frankly, this is some spectacular talking out of your arse."

Anthony's chest puffed out and Sarah put down her fork, covering her face with one hand.

"You find out Fran's bi, so you sack him. You find out you have a daughter instead of a son—"

"Don't be ridic—"

"So you try and kick me out," Jim finished loudly.

"You've come into my home and you've done nothing but advertise your lifestyle—"

"And you don't?" Jim snapped. "You come home, you kiss your wife in front of me. Your kids are here, kids that look like a combination of the two of you. This house is a shrine to the fact you're both straight. Your lifestyle. And if yours is allowed in here, why isn't mine?"

Sarah put down her fork and started to shake her head.

"And now you think my advertising my lifestyle has made Charlotte a girl, but you've been advertising yours a lot longer around her than I have, so either I am really, *really* good at this or it's bollocks."

"It doesn't matter."

Sarah cut across them both in a quavering voice.

"It doesn't matter. Os—Charlotte has told us the truth and we have to deal with it and support her—"

"I called Reverend Marsh after the sermon today and he suggested a counsellor in—"

"I am not sending my son to a conversion therapist!" Sarah shrieked.

Her plate crashed under her fist. The crockery jumped. Aggie let out a startled wail.

"Don't you dare," she croaked. "I am not—no. *No.* I'm not—I know enough to know that those people are—are—"

She glanced at the children and fell quiet, biting her lip.

"He can *help*—"

"No," Sarah said. "It's torture. It's not help. It's—it's horrible, it's abusive and horrible and I am not sending *any* of my children to people like that."

"For goodness' sake, Sarah, it's just some silly, childish confusion—Harry says the man's very good and can help fix—"

"*I said no!*"

She screamed it. Aggie began to cry. Jim felt frozen in place, awed by the look of fury on Sarah's face.

"There's nothing to fix!" she shouted. "Don't you dare tell me that my s—my daughter needs fixing! My brother doesn't need fixing and my s—daughter doesn't need fixing and don't you *dare*, Anthony! Don't you dare! If you even *try* to send Oscar — send Charlotte to that man, I'll take the kids, *all* of them, and we'll be gone before you even figure out what happened, you selfish, stupid son of a bitch!"

And just like that, she was back.

Jim's big sister. Screaming arguments and slamming doors on Mum when they were teenagers. Bawling him out when he got arrested. Clipping him round the ear outside school when she was tasked with getting him home and he wanted to go and play on his bike with his mates. Same squawking voice. Same unstoppable force.

Jim's heart flushed with warmth. So she was still there. Under the heels and the lace and the proper church wife look and the *disapproval*. The pompous, holier-than-thou, wannabe middle-class *approval*.

She'd finally bared her teeth and Jim had never been so fucking glad to see her.

"Her name is Charlotte and she's our daughter and if that — if that makes her better, if that makes her happy, then I don't damn well care!" Sarah bellowed. "And I need Jim here! He knows what to do and I don't! So you can get your head out of your arse for once in your life, you insufferable *idiot*, and do as you're told by your wife for once instead of your precious Reverend Marsh!"

Jim pushed back from his seat.

He'd sat through too many of these rows before. Too many attempts at blaming other people and finding cures. It had been Mum for him, but Anthony sounded very much the same, and Jim couldn't be bothered listening to the same recycled shit.

"Come on," he said to Charlotte. "Let's get some ice cream and you can tell me about your latest book, huh?"

She jumped up, white-faced and tight-lipped. Her fingers were shredding a napkin and Jim felt a vicious surge of anger against her father.

"I don't want you going anywhere with my son."

The retort was sharp. Firm. Deep.

"He'll stay right here and we are going to fix this. Fix him."

Jim stopped.

In the doorway, hand on Charlotte's shoulder, he just stopped. Then he patted it and said, "Hang on a sec, kid."

By the time he turned round, every muscle in his body was grinding.

He felt like he was that bratty kid again. He felt like he had the night it all went wrong. Like he could throw one punch and end the world, like he was invincible and needed the blood on his knuckles to prove it. He could cave Anthony's face in with one blow. Could end any influence this lethargic God-botherer could have over the rest of Charlotte's life, or Jim's.

But he felt older, too. He felt a tight coil of control around every fibre as he paced across the carpet to Anthony's chair and leaned down. He braced his weight on the table, right over Anthony's plate, and leaned in.

So close, he could see the flecks of black in wide brown eyes.

"Don't."

Silence.

The whole room held its breath. Even Patricia had gone still. Anthony stared back at him, his mouth open and lower lip wobbling like a frightened child.

"Don't," Jim repeated. "Don't you ever — *ever* — talk about my niece like that again."

A flicker of weak indignation appeared. It came and went like lightning and the protest might have sounded pompous and aggressive, once upon a time. But instead it flapped out through shaking lips, like a loose sail in a heavy wind.

"He is my — "

"She. Is. My. *Niece.*"

Anthony's mouth worked. But nothing came out. Jim felt everything creak — back, shoulders, table, floor — as he straightened up. The plates bounced as he stepped back and he broke eye contact only at the last second, turning at the door to squeeze Charlotte's shoulder.

"Come on," he said. "Let's hit the road."

He didn't have car keys, but he did have his phone, a set of earphones and a Spotify list. And — of course — a good spot on the garden wall to watch the stars. There was an owl hooting peaceably in a nearby tree, totally untroubled, and for a little while, they sat in the dark together, Charlotte sniffling under his arm quietly before she dried her eyes and reached for the spare earbud dangling down his chest.

"I don't like this song," she mumbled.

"Find a different one, then. No Disney shit."

"Disney's great."

"I don't think so, brat. I'll push you off this wall."

"No, you won't."

She forced him through a couple of ball-shrinkingly shrill musical numbers that Jim couldn't *swear* were

Disney, but strongly suspected. Eventually, though, she found her way into his more obscure folders and stumbled on *Odds Are*. Its upbeat rhythm made her pause and Jim crooned away to it in the quiet. Eventually, Charlotte opened up and sang with him. They looped the same song, over and over again until it was probably driving the local wildlife nuts, but Jim didn't care. If he could get one thing into her head, *Odds Are* was a good pick. Even if they were mutually terrible at the required American accent. Or singing anything at all, actually.

Eventually, he heard the crunch of gravel in a pause as the song reset itself and he handed over his earbud to Charlotte before twisting around to stare down at — thankfully — Sarah. Just Sarah. Standing in the cold, hugging herself and the glimmer of tears perfectly visible in the starlight.

"It's past bedtime," she said softly.

"I know."

"Come down. Both of you."

Jim sighed and tapped Charlotte on the shoulder. She twisted and slid down with obvious reluctance and visibly hesitated when Sarah raised her arms. But then, to Jim's surprise, Sarah simply stepped forward and hugged her anyway, burying her face into Charlotte's hair and squeezing tight.

And, slowly, Charlotte hugged back.

A savage lump rose in Jim's throat. He'd never had that hug. Him and Mum had bawled each other out and never spoken again. From what he gathered, Fran had been much the same. In a weird way, Jim had never really believed in supportive families. He'd never known someone with parents who'd been on board. He'd never met someone who took their boyfriend home to meet their mum. Christ, were things actually different? Could things really be like that? Was he finally getting on a bit—or was Charlotte just lucky?

He glanced at the house, at the missing space where her father ought to have been, and figured she was probably just lucky.

"Don't listen to your dad," Sarah whispered hoarsely. "You're not going anywhere."

Then she looked up at Jim, her stare freezing him solid in the moonlight.

"And neither are you."

Chapter Twenty

Me: Have you left work?

Fran: Just getting in the car, why?

Me: Come over.

Fran: To your sister's?

Me: Yeah.

There was a short pause.

Fran: Is that a good idea?

Jim blew upward into his hair. No? But then, he needed to know.

Me: Anthony's at church. Sarah bawled him out at dinner yesterday, proper screamed in his face.

Fran: You're plotting something.

Fran: Tell me what or I'm going home.

Me: Dick

Fran: Later

Jim smirked but didn't rise to it.

Me: I want to have you over and just...be normal but obviously with you, you know? Just hug on the sofa in front of a film. Be like married people get to be. And make Anthony and Sarah see it, make the kids see it and I want to see what she does.

In truth, he wanted to test her. He wanted to know she was finally changing her tune. He wanted to know the shock of her own little family turning out to be rainbow-coloured, too, was actually going to stick and make Sarah act like she should have been for all those years with him. He wanted to know she'd stand up to Anthony not just the one time, but twice—and he wanted to know that Anthony would be beaten twice, too.

Because, ultimately, Jim couldn't stay. The atmosphere was oppressive, the tension so thick it could not only be cut with a knife but used to build a new extension out of invisible bricks. He needed air, he needed space—and, aside from all the mess, he wanted Fran. He wanted to spend more time with him, not shuffling between two places all the time and losing out to Fran's day job and other students. Even if all he saw was a sleepy face over dinner and a body next to his in bed in the night.

But it meant leaving Charlotte behind.
And Jim couldn't just do that.

Fran: Promise no punching people?

Me: Promise!

Fran: Okay.

Jim grinned and rocked himself up from the bed. He'd spent the day out in town job-hunting again and it was blisteringly hot. The summer holidays were coming and he couldn't wait. Fran worked long and boring hours and Jim was fully intending to steal him over the six-week break. Dating a teacher sucked.

He headed downstairs to reserve the living room — or rescue it from marauding children. Patricia was in her lessons in the office, but Charlotte had been excused and he found her nose-deep in a book and Zoe playing with Aggie on the rug.

"Mind if I steal this room, ladies?" he asked, knocking loudly on the door frame. "Got a hot date with a pianist and we're going to watch a film."

Zoe and Aggie beat a retreat, but Charlotte whined to stay, wanting to know what film and if she could watch, too.

"Fran gets to pick the film," Jim said, "but you can stay if he says so."

Charlotte grinned. She plainly knew Fran to be a sucker, tutor or no tutor, and Jim rolled his eyes as he wandered off toward the kitchen to hunt out a bottle of wine. One glass for Fran, the rest for him. Maybe a cheeky measure for Charlotte, too, no harm in that.

His mobile started ringing just as he opened the fridge, and he sighed as he eased the phone out of his back pocket and jammed it into his shoulder, still squinting at the labels.

"Hello?"

"Hi, is that Jim Love?"

"Yeah."

"It's Ari Pekkanen, manager at the Bell. You came in this morning and talked to my colleague about work and left your CV with him."

Jim's stomach jumped.

"I have some vacancies behind the bar and in the restaurant area, are you still interested?"

"*Hell* yes."

Work. Fuck yes, *work.* He didn't care if it was part-time or shit hours or, hell, *zero* hours. It was work. Pubs were busy over the summer, so there'd be *some* money. It was easier to get more jobs once he had one job. And Jim had worked in pubs and bars before. It was just a case of not being a prick and turning up on time enough days in a row before more and more hours appeared, and the better shifts, and dumb titles like team leader or head waiter or whatever started popping up and the wage would inch above minimum. And once he was a team leader at something, he could start hunting up the jobs with *good* pay, then—

Then, hell. Then he could do a little bit more than just pay his share of Fran's bills.

He blindly agreed to go in for a trial run on Wednesday—"full shift but nothing too insane, what size shirt are you, show you round the place"—and hung up with such a huge grin on his face that when Sarah walked into the kitchen, she stopped dead.

"What's gotten into you?"

"New job."

"Oh."

To his surprise, she didn't seem pleased.

"What?" he said. "New job means I can get out of your hair."

Sarah leaned against the table, blowing out her cheeks. "I—I don't know I'm ready for that," she muttered.

Jim raised his eyebrows.

"I—just—you know. Os—Charlotte. Charlotte. And with Anthony being such a prick. I don't—he's—she's—I need you here, Jim."

Slowly, he turned to face her properly.

"You don't."

"But—!"

"You know what you have to do," Jim said. "Long as she knows you're going to support her as your daughter, just like you would Pat and Aggie—"

A flicker of intense disgust at his nicknames washed over his sister's face and Jim couldn't help but smirk. He hid it by opening the fridge and retrieving the wine bottle he'd been after.

"Then the rest of it isn't really all that different. Just listen to her while she figures stuff out. And I'm not going to vanish off the face of the earth."

"You never visited before," she said quietly.

"You never really made this somewhere I felt okay visiting."

She swallowed. "And—and now?"

"S'different now."

The buzzer went off in the hall. He rolled his eyes.

"It's Fran."

"Oh. Um. Date?"

"Yeah, we're gonna watch a movie in the living room and maybe go out for dinner later."

She nodded, chewing on her lip. The buzzer went off again and Jim set the bottle down, skirting around her to go and release it. As the light flashed green and he faintly heard the creak of the gates beginning to pull back at the end of the drive, Jim leaned against the hall wall, frowning at his feet.

What the hell to do?

Shrugging, he opened the door and walked out into the sun. The gravel was hot. The car was hotter when he leaned in the open window for a kiss and Fran's skin burned like the surface of the sun. He looked obnoxiously attractive in those mirrored sunglasses and his work suit and Jim wanted to sack off the whole idea and go back to his place for some fun instead.

Then Fran opened the door right into his gut and he doubled up, winded.

"That's what you get for being slow," he said imperiously, then stooped to kiss the crown of Jim's head. "That normally queer enough for you?"

"Prick," Jim grunted, gingerly straightening up. His sour look was met with a wide smile and it melted his defences. "Good day?"

"Decent enough and getting better by the minute. So where we headed?"

"Living room. Charlotte wants to gatecrash, so pick a suitable film."

Turned out Fran was into mocking the Transformers movies. Jim ended up squashed into the recliner with him, their bare feet all tangled up on the rest and a bony shoulder wedged under his armpit. The fair hair at his nose smelled like summer and sunshine and Jim found himself almost dozing as his niece and his boyfriend —

boring sods, the pair of them — talked musical scores. The wine was taking the edge off nicely and he could have napped.

Then the living room door opened and his sister's voice floated into his consciousness.

"Room for one more?"

He opened an eye. Sarah smiled uncertainly, then edged around the sofa and sat down next to Charlotte. She had a bowl.

"You brought popcorn?" Fran asked.

"Mhmm."

"I think we can fit you in."

Jim wasn't a popcorn fan but offered her a smile as the bowl was passed round. He'd never done this before. Never just lain in a chair having a cuddle with another bloke where his sister could see. They probably looked completely daft — Fran hadn't even taken off his waistcoat and Jim had been idly playing with one of the buttons for the better part of an hour — but although her eyes lingered for a little while, she soon relaxed and started to pay more attention to the film, even getting up to put the next one on when the credits rolled.

Then she said, "I hate to talk business, but — Fran?"

His name sounded odd from her lips and it obviously took a moment before Fran realised. When he did, he nearly put his elbow into Jim's sternum to push himself up a little.

"Sorry, Sarah. What is it?"

"Would you be willing to come back?"

Fran blinked. So did Jim. His jaw sagged as he stared at Sarah. Come back? Was she seriously —?

"I know Anthony called you and terminated the agreement, but — I don't agree. The children both did so well with you and liked your lessons so much. I'd be so appreciative if you'd be willing to come back and teach them again. And I'd raise your fee, you know."

Charlotte's face lit up. For a moment, Fran tensed all along Jim's side and he frowned.

Then relaxed.

Just like that.

"I'd be happy to. They're good kids."

"Can I learn the trumpet?" Charlotte burst out. "Like you played at Pride? Can I? Mum, say I can learn the trumpet!"

She probably hadn't meant it as a test, the way Jim had meant the evening to be one. But Sarah blinked as though searching for a correct answer, then folded herself back down on the sofa and picked up the remote control again.

"If you pass your next piano grading, then we'll have a talk about the trumpet."

Fran shifted onto his side. A hip came up to shadow Jim's. The weight on his side increased and a nose brushed the shell of his ear.

"Need the facilities," he said. "Get the rest of that wine while I'm up."

"You're driving," Jim said muzzily and Fran laughed.

"They're called taxis. Amazing things."

Then he was up, fingers trailing away from Jim's chest as if they didn't want to let go, and Jim sighed, levering himself out of his nest with difficulty to fetch the rest of the wine.

Sarah smiled at him.

Standing in the kitchen, holding a half-empty bottle in one hand, everything hit Jim in the chest like a freight train. He was twenty-six and, for the first time, he'd been able to hug his boyfriend in front of his family without—anything. Without judgement. Without criticism. Without spite and malice and hate. Just do it, because he wanted to, and get nothing out of them but a smile.

He lingered outside the downstairs bathroom and caught Fran by a belt loop when he emerged. Reeled him in for a kiss that tasted like red wine and warmth, sticky lips and soft skin. Jim patted that firm bum in tight suit trousers and was laughed at like they did this every evening of the week, in the exact same spot.

"Behave," Fran whispered.

Jim grinned.

"Make me."

Epilogue

There it was.

Jim lifted a hand and waved as the black Mercedes inched backward into a slightly-too-tight spot. It was gleaming. Anthony must have been up half the night cleaning it.

Of course, there was no sign of him. Sarah got out looking a million dollars in a little black dress and a pair of enormous Hepburn-esque sunglasses. The white sunhat did nothing to get rid of the impression, either, though the sensible flats watered down the effect. Jim snorted with laughter. What a Pride virgin.

He waved again and managed to catch her attention. She waved back and he pointed down the road to the parking meter. A thumbs-up and she trotted away.

Charlotte's eleven-year-old brain had no such concerns. She bounced out of the passenger seat like a rubber ball and shot across the road, her case in one hand and her flower necklace from last year in the other. It was a bit dusty but still plenty colourful and she flung it over Jim's neck.

"For safekeeping," she explained.

"Right you are." He raised his eyebrows. "Er. What are you wearing?"

Insta-scowl.

"My new skirt!"

"That's a belt."

"Oh my God, you're as bad as Mum," she sneered with a spectacular eye-roll.

"And I am emigrating to Timbuktu when you hit twelve because holy f — hell."

"Holy fuck," Charlotte corrected smugly.

"Sarah!"

"Don't!" she whined.

Sarah cupped her ear. Jim shook his head and waved her off.

"I hate you," Charlotte sulked.

"Whatever, kid. C'mon. Let's go find the band."

They weren't hard to find. There was only ten minutes to go and a couple of the trombonists were warming up already. Not, in this sticky heat, that Jim believed for a second anything needed warming up. There'd been a thunderstorm brewing for weeks and the air was heavy and oppressive. He'd not even had sex in a fortnight. It was just too damn hot to touch and it was *torture.*

He dropped Charlotte off with the youth section, rolling his eyes as she turned her back and pretended he didn't exist in favour of smiling shyly at a black girl he strongly suspected was the constantly mentioned Hayley. Ever since she'd joined the queer music group, it had been Hayley this and Hayley that and well, *Hayley* says.

He was fed up of Hayley and what she said. God only knew how her poor mother felt.

He found Sarah back at the car and they slid into the throngs either side of the parade to watch. The sun beat down on them and he grudgingly submitted to her mothering instinct and let her slap suncream on his neck. She *did* slap, too, and he whined at her.

"Oh, give over," she said. "You're as bad as Patricia."

"Harsh."

She rolled her eyes, then hesitated. "Jim."

"Oh God. I have the right to remain silent."

"Be *serious*."

He sobered up.

"How — how am I doing? Honestly?"

Jim stared at her. She was dressed for a wedding, not a Pride parade. She got tense and uncomfortable whenever a nearly naked guy got anywhere near them. She was probably going to faint if one of those topless feminist protesters walked past. Her entire look *screamed* someone's cisgender, straight relative. Someone who was way out of her depth in a very rough sea and had only just learned how to swim.

"You're here," he said simply.

She stared right back.

"You're *here*, Sarah. How do you think you're doing?"

She nodded jerkily, taking a shaky breath. Then she leaned over the barrier to peer at the front of the parade. "So, do they usually start on time, or —"

"Bloody Pride virgins," Jim said. He waved at a vendor. "Hey! Hey, pal! Over here. Lady needs some colour on this funeral gear."

"How dare you," the vendor said. "The lady looks fabulous! You, on the other hand, would look better without this lot. What are you doing later?"

"One of the marchers, sorry."

"No room for a little one?"

"I'm the jealous type." Jim grinned and hooked a flower necklace over Sarah's head. She giggled girlishly and let the guy mark her face with a couple of rainbow flags from a colourful wax block.

"It's *always* the pretty women," he said mournfully. "You *sure* you couldn't be persuaded over to my side? You'd make a gorgeous man, you know. Look at them legs!"

Once, she'd have slapped him. Jim's chest burned as she just giggled again and waved him off. "Sorry," she said. "Proud mum."

"Oh dear," he clucked. "Well, good on you, sweetie."

He sashayed away as one of the floats belted out some Ariana Grande and lurched into motion. The sunny smile dipped a little at the nearly naked bondage guys and Jim had to chew on a knuckle to stop himself from collapsing into fits when she saw a couple of young policemen doing a very lively, very camp waltz down the middle of the road and being serenely filmed by their completely unfazed, blatantly heterosexual sergeant.

Then came the marching band.

Sarah squealed and held up her phone when Charlotte came into view. Her eyes were trained resolutely on her sheet and Jim knew exactly what she was playing even over the din, as she'd been practising for weeks. She didn't dance like some of the more confident players—but she was in step with her precious Hayley and when Jim roared her name, she did glance up, just once, to look at them.

And beamed at her mum, just in time for the picture.

"Perfect," Sarah said.

Jim leaned over. It was. "You should put it up on the wall."

For a split second, Sarah paused.

Then she said, "Yes. Yes, you're right. Right in the hall."

Jim squeezed her arm. "You're doing fine."

Sarah swallowed.

"So's Charlotte."

"She is, isn't she?"

There was the faintest hint of a real question and Jim slung an arm over her shoulders and hugged her.

"She is," he promised.

"Anthony — Anthony called her Charlie last night."

Jim paused.

"I mean, she hated it. She goes spare when the kids at her riding club do it. But...you know. He's trying. He'll —"

There was a very long pause.

"He might get there, you know."

Jim knocked his head lightly against hers.

"Maybe there's some hope for the old bastard yet."

"Hey!"

"Hey, *you* married him. *I* reserve the right to think he's a tool."

They bickered until the band passed out of sight, then Sarah clutched her handbag and frowned at those yet to come.

"I don't know this is my thing," she said eventually. "It's very noisy, isn't it?"

"Yeah. C'mon. Let's get in before the big crowds and find a good picnic spot for Charlotte to studiously avoid until Hayley leaves."

Sarah rolled her eyes. "Oh my goodness, that girl! I never thought I'd say this, but, honestly, I wish Charlotte would just ask her out and stop this silly nonsense."

Jim tuned her out as they tossed their donation fee in the buckets and wandered into the park. It was already busy, but not the heaving chaos of post-parade. They found a spot, then he talked Sarah into a half pint of lager, promising it would wear off before Charlotte let them leave if she was going to flirt with Hayley all day, and stretched out in the sun to watch the eye candy go by and the storm clouds gather in the sky.

God, this was the life.

He'd go get dinner with the girls, then head back out to recapture Fran in his high heels and glitter in some nightclub somewhere. And he was going to have to get a picture because Charlotte didn't believe her beloved suit-wearing music tutor was so garish as to wear high heels and glitter. And he'd wake up in the morning feeling like death warmed over and they'd probably have a feel-better shag on the new sofa in the afternoon when they'd both stopped throwing up.

"Hey, Sarah."

"What?"

"Can you keep a secret?"

"I know your sorts of secret, James Love, I don't want to know."

"Oh, trust me, you have *no* idea."

"Good. But go on, then."

"D'you reckon Fran's the marrying kind?"

She snorted. "Jimmy, I don't think *you're* the marrying kind."

"Yeah, but if."

"I think you're besotted."

"I know *that*," Jim said. "Question is, is *he* besotted."

"I'd say so. He puts up with you, doesn't he?"

Jim rolled his eyes at the clouds.

"Give it more than a year," she advised and Jim grinned. Maybe they could have a long engagement. "You're good together, you know. You and Fran."

"Glad to hear it."

Jim jumped at the new voice and lifted his shades to grin. Haloed by the sun, Fran was an ivory tower of the best kind. His glasses had been exchanged for heavy mirrored shades, but they were dark blots atop his white hair as he smiled down at them. Despite the heat, he was in his waistcoat, shirtsleeves rolled to the elbow, his new tattoo snaking away up his elbow and disappearing into the white. His top button was open and the very lip of the same ink could *just* be seen in the shadows of the V. Jim might have to look later. Just to check it was healing nicely and all. After four months.

"You coming down or am I coming up?" Jim asked.

"That you are even allowed to speak to the likes of me is a sign you're going up in the world, sweetheart," Fran said loftily, but then he dropped to his knees and smeared grass stains on his suit without a care. He'd brought offerings. A kiss and a bottle of Grolsch. Jim grinned.

"Yes, yes, you are the sun at the centre of the universe, and I a small rocky planet orbiting your magnificence."

"After last night's curry, try a gas planet."

Sarah laughed. "I'll go and find a first aid kit for that burn, should I, Jim?"

"I hate the pair of you," Jim whined.

Fran nipped his ear and smirked, settling down on the grass beside him and hooking a leg over Jim's, close and intimate and very, very huggable. And other things.

"Did you see Charlotte?" Sarah fussed.

"Yeah, she was busy flirting with Hayley at the end of the march," Fran said.

"So she got into the park? I might ring her —"

"Yes, she was inside."

"And don't," Jim advised. "She wants to just have a nice day flirting with her crush, let her. She's a kid, they won't let her back out of the gates without an adult. She's safe in here. And she's only got, what, a tenner? It's not going to go very far in here, she'll find us sooner or later."

He stretched back out on the grass. The sun had gone behind the clouds, but the air was hot and heavy and Fran hotter and heavier where he leaned against Jim's ribs and talked music with Sarah. Occasionally, young voices yelled, "Hi, Mr Carr!" and Jim felt an arm lift in a wave, but otherwise he tuned out the world to bask in peace. Next week, they'd move into their new house together and Jim needed to store up all his energy. New houses needed christening, after all. And — oh yeah.

He sat up again and butted his head against Fran's neck lightly. "Hey."

"What?"

"Come to the leather tent with me."

"What, now?"

"Yeah. It'll only take a few minutes."

They left their things with Sarah and Jim slid a hand into Fran's back pocket so they staggered in step across the field. People milled about, the march having spilled en masse into the park, and Fran lifted his shades back to the top of his head as they passed voice after voice, teenager after teenager, yelling, "Hi, Mr Carr!" in his direction.

"Gay as fuck, your school."

"All part of the big homosexual agenda," Fran quipped.

"What, convert them all?"

"Yeah, makes up for the lack of having kids."

Jim laughed as they reached the tent, and pointed out the wheels he'd seen online. Little spikes that left a prickling trail and Fran shivered just like he'd hoped when he ran one down a bare arm.

"So, can I try it?"

Fran licked his lips. "You remember ages ago — like, when we first got together — you wanted to try a game with a blindfold and a gag and the flat of a cold knife?"

Jim stared.

"Do you still want to?"

"Oh my God, yes."

Fran wiggled the little wheel in his hand.

"Let's start with this."

"*God*, yes."

They found a new blindfold, too, and Jim was laughed at for hopefully suggesting a very attractive pair of cuffs. He pouted, but it got him nothing but a kiss and a smacked arse, then he was dragged back out onto the field by the hand, their paper bag of goodies under one arm and an angel hot enough to burn his fingers clean off towing him in a blazing wake.

"Wait! Wait, wait, wait —"

"*What?*" Fran demanded impatiently.

"Phone!"

But it was just a text. From Her Majesty, somewhere in the chaos.

Lottie!: Can you say someone's your girlfriend if you've not been on a date yet?

"Oh, hello," Fran said, grinning over his shoulder.
"What do you reckon?" Jim asked.
"Depends if a date has been agreed to."

Me: If she's said yes to going on a date then yes.

Lottie!: Can I borrow a tenner?

Me: Is it for dating purposes?

Lottie!: Yeah :)

Me: Then yes, and say hi to Hayley for us.

Lottie!: OMFG :((((

Fran cackled with laughter and Jim caught his chin, hooking it up for a sharp kiss.

"Hey," he whispered. "She's good, Sarah can wait for a few minutes — want to take this off into the trees for some good old Pride tradition?"

"You filthy bastard," Fran breathed, rising on his toes and sealing their lips once more. His hands caught in Jim's hair. Stroked. Seized.

And the thunder exploded.

The heavens opened. Rain like a burst river crashed down. People started screaming and running for the tents — and Jim laughed into the searing kiss, winding both arms around Fran's hips and hauling him ever closer.

"On second thought," he breathed, stroking down Fran's neck with his nose and finding a soft pulse, warm and steady, to kiss instead. "I'm good right here."

"You're never good."

"Behave," Jim chided.

A gentle laugh. A mere whisper through the downpour and crashing thunder.

"Make me."

Jim stroked his hand through wet hair and cupped the back of his head. Drew him in. Silenced the next breath with a kiss like they were drowning, and never wanted to let go.

Now was the time for his best behaviour.

Want to see more from this author? Here's a taster for you to enjoy!

Enough
Matthew J. Metzger

Excerpt

He could smell the fire.

He was blind. His eyes streamed. The curling wallpaper crackled and hissed. His skin was burning. The air in his lungs seared him from the inside out. And there was nowhere to go — no escape from the heat, no escape from the orange towers and acrid black smoke, no *air*.

"Ezra!"

The smoke wrapped itself around his teeth and tongue like a grotesque mockery of a kiss, and there was no reply but the roar of hot air and climbing fire. The house was burning. *The house was burning!*

"Ezra! *Ez!*"

A scream. A piercing scream, like nothing he'd ever heard, but before he could move, the wooden boards crumbled to ash and he was falling, tearing through the shreds of stairs into the inferno, and —

Jesse hit the carpet with a thump and jarred himself awake.

The flat was quiet. The streetlight touched the other side of the curtains with a faint orange light. There was no smoke, no fire, no sound. Nothing.

Jesse dragged himself back onto the bed. The sheets were impossibly tangled and his tank top stuck to him with sweat. His wrist ached in its brace where he'd bumped it, but the panic hadn't quite eased its grip on his heart or his lungs, and he fumbled for his phone, ignoring the pain.

Thank God for speed dial.

The clock on the side said two-fifty-eight, and the phone rang six times before the line coughed and crackled and a sleepy voice, tinged in the early hours with the fading edges of a Welsh accent, mumbled a vague sort of question.

"Ez?"

There was a rustle of sheets. "Jesse?"

"Oh, God," Jesse breathed. The air escaped in a rush, loud and hard. His lungs shook with the effort. "Shit. I just— I needed to check—"

"Jess? What's happened, sweetheart?"

The soft roll of his vowels, the accent entirely muted when he was properly awake, was as comforting as a hug, and Jesse coughed out, "Nightmare," before thinking twice. Ezra was okay. He was okay. It was all okay.

"Oh, sweetheart," Ezra murmured, low and crooning. "Do you want to tell me about it?"

"I need—can I come over? I know it's late and I know you have work in the morning, but—I just—I need—"

"No," Ezra interrupted, and Jesse's stomach twisted violently.

"*Please*, Ez, I—"

"Hey, hey, hey." Ezra cut him off. "Hey, stop, calm down, sweetheart. I *meant* you can't come here. You don't sound okay, not to me, and I don't want you to go out like this, so I'll come to you, all right?"

Jesse exhaled, the twist easing. "Okay."

"You okay if I hang up, or do you want me to put the phone on speaker?"

"Can—speaker," Jesse swallowed against the nausea. He was still shaking, he realised faintly. "I just—I couldn't find you, Ez. The house was burning and I couldn't find you, and I—I need to hear you. You don't have to talk to me, but I need to hear you."

"Okay." The phone crackled again and clunked, and suddenly Ezra's voice was loud and echoing. *Soothing.* The Welsh hint was fading, and Jesse could suddenly hear him dressing, but he was *there*. "Was it my house or the one last week?"

"Yours," Jesse said. "I was on the stairs, and they gave way, and I woke up. I couldn't find you."

"If my house was on fire, I would probably be in the kitchen having caused it," Ezra said, and yawned loudly. "Make yourself useful, sweetheart, and make up a brew for me? I've not slept long."

Jesse knew better than to apologise. He shrugged out of his sweat-soaked pyjamas and pulled on a pair of jogging bottoms before taking the phone through the narrow hall into the kitchen. The kitchen window overlooked the main road. A police car trailed idly by on the prowl. Phone to his ear, he listened to Ezra swear sleepily at his cupboard, and the soft sounds of those narrow feet padding downstairs.

"Sweetheart?"

"Mm?" Jesse listened to the front door and the heavy sound of the key.

"I'm going to hang up while I drive. You all right for ten minutes until I get there?"

"Yeah," Jesse croaked. His heart had come down out of the rafters, and he could breathe. The streetlights didn't look threatening anymore. He just felt…shaky. Sick and shaky and scared. "Yeah, Ez, I'll be fine."

"Okay. Love you."

The dial tone was immediate. Jesse dropped the phone to the counter and switched on the kettle, staring out of the window and waiting, arms folded against the chill. It wasn't the first nightmare, and it wouldn't be the last. He usually managed one a week without fail, and the injury hadn't helped matters. But they didn't usually involve Ezra in burning buildings. They didn't usually involve losing him.

And Jesse couldn't stomach the thought of losing him.

Which was a bit scary in itself. They'd only met eight months ago. At a gay bar, of all places — the one place where he went to meet sex partners, not *partner* partners. Jesse had thought the freckled blond with the dark eyes was pretty in the neon lights and had bought him a drink, talked him into a dance, bought him another. Kissed him at the back of the dance floor — and had promptly found himself alone, but with a phone number in his back pocket.

He'd wanted sex. That was all he'd been after. Sex with a pretty guy. But then they'd gone on a date and he'd met Ezra *properly*, and he was lost. Ezra wasn't just a handsome face and nice legs. Ezra was the world. He was *Jesse's* world, and it had only been eight months, but Jesse still knew that this was it, for him. Ezra was it. There would never be anyone else like him.

So he stood in a tense vigil at the window, waiting for the faithful little Peugeot 207 to creep around the corner. Waiting for Ezra to come, because there was emotional shock and there was sense, and the two weren't in line right now. He *knew* Ezra was okay. He knew it. He'd answered the phone. He'd been sleepy and understanding and sworn at his cupboard. He was fine.

But Jesse still needed to reach out and touch him, just to make sure. *Somehow.*

The little blue car was lonely on the three-in-the-morning road, and Jesse propped the door of his flat to creep down the communal stairs and open the main door. Ezra had gotten sort-of dressed, in jeans and an open check shirt, feet shoved into his trainers without socks, and his hair was wild and fluffy, in gleeful disarray, as he locked the car and wrapped himself around Jesse in a tight, warm hug.

Jesse clung back until something creaked, and pressed the side of his face against that wild hair.

"You're all right, sweetheart," Ezra murmured.

Jesse squeezed again until Ezra's grip on the nape of his neck tightened in warning, then he let go and dragged Ezra up the silent stairs by the hand. Concrete stairs. They wouldn't collapse in a fire until the whole building came down.

He didn't say a word until he'd pressed the requested tea into Ezra's hands, locked the door again and bundled them both back to the messy bed. Ezra was equally silent, taking a couple of mouthfuls before abandoning the tea, stripping to his underwear and crawling into the mess to mould himself into Jesse's arms.

"There you go," he murmured lowly, kissing Jesse's encroaching stubble and stroking a hand gently through his hair. "Feel better now?"

"Mm," Jesse pressed his nose into Ezra's neck, tangling their legs together. He could feel a strong pulse in Ezra's jugular. He could feel the rough skin of the bumpy scar on Ezra's shoulder under his fingertips. He could feel the fuzzy mess of Ezra's hair, usually styled and stiff in that messy-but-it's-on-purpose-so-it's-okay manner, now just loose and wild. He could feel *him*. "Thank you."

"Thank me again tomorrow afternoon when I'm grumpy and exhausted after two hours of the Year Nines."

"Okay," Jesse agreed, sliding his arms completely around Ezra's back until he enveloped him. They didn't often sleep cuddled together — or even together at all, between Ezra's eight-to-four and Jesse's shifts — but he needed this. He *needed* it.

"Mind if I go to sleep?"

"No," Jesse squirmed until Ezra got the hint and tucked his head under his chin. His hair tickled. Jesse kissed the top of his head and wished he had the easy grace with language that Ezra did. Wished he could express himself properly. Wished he could talk as easily as he hugged. But all that came out was, "I just needed to touch you."

Ezra said nothing to that, simply shifting until he was comfortable, one arm over Jesse's ribs and the other tucked over his own waist in a casual sort of drop. Ezra was *long* — long limbs, long neck, all willowy lines and bendy joints, and he settled like water into the bulkier, stiffer contours of Jesse's body.

But he fit, and he fit perfectly, and Jesse wrapped him up and held him, breathing in the smell of store-brand shampoo and cheap aftershave until the last traces of the nightmare-induced fear washed away.

It was still a long time before he slept.

* * * *

Bzt, bzt, bzt, bzt —

Jesse swatted at the noise, and a low laugh and blessed quiet were his reply. "Urgh," he said.

"Mm," Ezra agreed. "But some of us have jobs to go to."

"I have a job," Jesse grumbled, still refusing to open his eyes.

"They just don't want you," Ezra teased, and Jesse cracked open an eye to glower at him. He'd *escaped*. He was standing by the bed buttoning the spare shirt he kept in Jesse's wardrobe. *Bastard.*

"C'mere." Jesse made grabby hands. Ezra stepped back.

"No," he said. "It's already quarter past. It's just as well I brought the car."

Jesse blinked up at him and stretched luxuriously. He'd not gone to sleep until half-four, wrapped around Ezra like a blanket, and he knew for a fact Ezra hadn't slept deeply either.

"It was a bad night," Jesse said eventually. "You should call in sick."

"And let some poor ineffectual supply teacher get a test tube shoved somewhere painful by the more creative ones? I don't think so." Ezra buttoned his collar and bent over the bed to kiss Jesse's hair. "But it's the last day. And after that, you get me all day and every day until occupational health clear you to go back to work."

Jesse caught his shoulder and sat up, deepening the kiss until Ezra sat gingerly on the edge of the mattress. He smelled of Jesse's shower gel and his hair was damp in its mousse-induced style. Ezra had very light, almost wispy hair. He'd used to spray it into its perfectly-styled, deliberately messy cloud until Jesse had come along and vetoed the flammable spray. The mousse wouldn't burst into flames, and it had the added bonus of not feeling so disgusting.

"Get your hands off that," Ezra murmured, and Jesse ran his hands down his back instead. "Mm. Jesse, I need to go."

"In a bit," Jesse coaxed, kissing his neck. He knew better than to bite above the collar — Ezra had nearly strangled him the one and only time he'd done that — but he couldn't resist open-mouthed kisses down the length of lightly freckling skin. The hot spring was taking its toll. "In a bit!" he added when Ezra began to push at him, and he tried to hang on, but Ezra did *yoga*, the bendy little savage, and escaped without so much as a struggle.

"I said *no*," he reiterated sternly, before grinning, kissing the top of Jesse's head and pushing him back onto the mattress. "Get some sleep and come and catch me after work. It's their last day, so make sure you turn up with the biggest bottle of whisky you can afford."

"Yessir," Jesse grinned, mouth still tingling, then Ezra was gone, shutting the bedroom door behind him. Jesse listened in mute love to the off-key singing as Ezra put his shoes on and clattered with keys — then the front door closed and the flat was silent.

It was April. The sun was high already, and the sky a deep, clear blue. Jesse could hear the sea from his flat in the winter, but in the spring it was too sedate to be picked out over the rush-hour traffic and the wail of an ambulance siren flying down the main road to the hospital. He bathed luxuriously in the light washing across the bed until he heard the cough and rumble of Ezra's car disappear into the melee of suits and drones going to work, and — finally — Jesse swung himself out of bed and faced the day.

Jesse was twenty-five and had had the same flat since he was seventeen. It was a *box*, Ezra insisted, but then Ezra had a degree and a last name that replaced 'I' with 'Y' because that looked fancier. Jesse was just Jesse Kevin Dawkins, and a box was all he needed. The kitchen was too small to close the door properly, the bathroom was the sort where taking a crap and washing his feet in the shower and hands in the sink at the same time was wholly possible, and the bedroom had a double bed with absolutely no floor space whatsoever. He'd had to take the door off the cupboard to fit the bed.

But it was *his* flat. Jesse had spent most of his childhood being bounced from place to place with his mother, and to have somewhere that was *his* was a big deal. Ezra could call it a box all he liked, but the only way Jesse was moving was if the flat burned down, or Ezra wanted them to live together.

Then they'd make a new home. The two of them.

It was a bit early for it, Jesse reflected as he jammed bread into the toaster and rummaged through the fridge for the grapefruit juice, but maybe once their anniversary arrived he could ask Ezra to live with him. Even if it meant bringing the stupid cats, and a whole bathroom counter of Ezra's hair products. All fifteen billion of them.

His phone buzzed on the counter where he'd abandoned it last night, and he smiled when he slid it open and Ezra's name popped up, cheerfully bright in the shimmering morning.

Ezra <3: Oh my God, one of the little shits has slashed the tyres on the head's car! Do I laugh or look mad like the rest of them?

Jesse laughed.

Me: Look mad. You look stunning when you laugh and that physics teacher has a thing for you. Don't encourage her!

Ezra <3: Sap ;) Love you too x

His heart hiccupped, and Jesse clutched the phone like a brainless newlywed until the toaster popped.

PUBLISHING

Sign up for our newsletter and find out about all our romance book releases, eBook sales and promotions, sneak peeks and FREE romance books!

About the Author

Matthew J. Metzger is an asexual, transgender British author juggling books, an office job and a love of travel with the human need for sleep once in a while. He writes both adult and young adult books focusing on LGBT+ characters and their relationships, particularly those from the less salubrious areas in which he was dragged up over the years.

On the very rare occasions that Matt isn't writing, he can usually be found at the gym, halfway up a mountain or collecting new tattoos. (And yes, he does have book ink…)

Matthew loves to hear from readers. You can find his contact information, website details and author profile page at http://www.pride-publishing.com